"Drive," Stacey breathed. "Please."

"The least I can do," the guy said as he put his foot to the floor and she felt a wrench as the force of acceleration pulled her back. She let out a gasp and automatically grabbed the seat belt.

"It's okay. You're safe with me," he said, looking round at her as he put more distance between them and Decker's.

I'm safe with no man, she thought to herself, but she said nothing, only stared out o   window at the blurry urban scene

"It's okay. Try to relax. I'm taking y   o get checked out."

Stacey squeezed her eyes shut a   ad. Why did men always think they k

"Seriously I don't want to go to a   n't need a bunch of X-rays."

"You don't know what you need   . You never did."

She jolted as if she'd been hit by the car all over again. She turned to face the guy—one eyebrow shot up in a way she knew so well. And then it all fell into place. Her heart pulsed right up into her throat.

Like a shutter opening on an old reel of film, Stacey watched helplessly as scene after scene of sunshine, pleasure and then hard, dark pain flashed through her mind. Marco Borsatto. The boy from the right side of the tracks, the boy she'd fallen helplessly in love with. The boy she'd thought had fallen helplessly in love with her.

Claimed by a Billionaire

*Commanding and charismatic, these men
take what—and who—they want!*

Dante Hermida, polo player and playboy
extraordinaire, meets the only woman
to tame him in

The Argentinian's Virgin Conquest
April 2017

Billionaire tycoon Marco Borsatto has never
forgiven Stacey Jackson's betrayal, but
he's never forgotten their chemistry...
Meeting her again, he's determined that
this time, she will never forget him!

The Italian's Vengeful Seduction
May 2017

You won't want to miss this dramatically intense,
scorchingly sexy duet from Bella Frances!

Bella Frances

THE ITALIAN'S VENGEFUL SEDUCTION

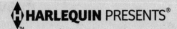
HARLEQUIN PRESENTS®

Recycling programs
for this product may
not exist in your area.

ISBN-13: 978-0-373-06068-9

The Italian's Vengeful Seduction

First North American Publication 2017

Copyright © 2017 by Bella Frances

www.Harlequin.com

Printed in U.S.A.

Unable to sit still without reading, **Bella Frances** first found romantic fiction at the age of twelve, in between deadly dull knitting patterns and recipes in the pages of her grandmother's magazines. An obsession was born! But it wasn't until one long, hot summer, after completing her first degree in English literature, that she fell upon the legends that are Harlequin books. She has occasionally lifted her head out of them since to do a range of jobs, including barmaid, financial adviser and teacher, as well as to practice (but never perfect) the art of motherhood to two (almost grown-up) cherubs.

Bella lives a very energetic life in the UK but tries desperately to travel for pleasure at least once a month—strictly in the interests of research!

Catch up with her on her website at bellafrances.co.uk.

Books by Bella Frances

Harlequin Presents

The Playboy of Argentina
The Scandal Behind the Wedding

Claimed by a Billionaire

The Argentinian's Virgin Conquest

Harlequin KISS

Dressed to Thrill

Visit the Author Profile page at Harlequin.com for more titles.

For
my hero, my Julian.

CHAPTER ONE

STACEY JACKSON WAS *nobody's* plaything. She reminded herself of that as she pressed a knuckle to the corner of her left eye and stopped dead the spring of hot, fat tears that swelled there. She was nobody's plaything and she was nobody's fool. And she was *not* going to apologise to any man—best customer included—for saying so.

So she'd lose her job. Again. But she was getting tired of Decker's Casino anyway. The late nights, the long shifts, the Perma-smile—being a croupier was exhausting.

And if that wasn't bad enough, being made to wear this stupid dress was the last straw.

If you could even call it that. Some strips of fabric held together by luck and pulled apart by filthy imaginations.

It made her look more like a hooker than Bruce's private dancers—which she'd told him as soon as she'd seen it. He'd told her to shut her mouth and get on with it. Which she had—she needed the money.

But the minute she'd leaned across the roulette wheel, right in front of him and his sleazy customers, she'd seen their hungry glances and felt a prickle of anger race up her spine. And then her mouth had gone into gear.

Didn't it always? And it always ended the same way.

Stacey lifted her finger and saw that her cats' eye liquid eyeliner was blurred now. She fished in the purse that dangled from her wrist, pulled out the pencil and slicked it back into place like the expert she was. Lipstick next—and then she stared at her face. The one that had got her into so much trouble over the years. She was twenty-six, and the hard times still weren't showing, but how much longer could she really expect to cash in on it? It had got her the job here at Decker's—and every other job before that. It wasn't that she *wanted* to look bad! But would it hurt for people to take her a little more seriously and see more than just a piece of ass and a pair of double Ds?

Her blue eyes flashed defiantly. Her father's eyes.

'You have to love yourself before anyone else will love you,' he had said. Easy for him. *His* last act of love had been to ruffle her hair, hop up into his trailer and take the interstate to As Far Away from Here as Possible.

Stacey bit down on her lip to scorch the memory. The last thing she could afford was any sentimentality. She was going to clear out right now. She wouldn't wait around to be fired. Bruce could roll his own damn dice. She'd walk out, collect her stuff from that crummy apartment and get a bus to New York City.

Why not? She'd tried her hand at Atlantic City, and she'd tried her hand on the cruise ships. There had to be somewhere in this world she'd fit in. Because one thing was for sure—there was no way she was going back to the End of the World, Long Island, until she'd done something to put the gossips in their place.

She pressed her lips together and checked her teeth for lipstick.

Yep, when she rolled back into Montauk she was going to be settled, sorted and sane. She was going to have a great job and a nice apartment. And a boyfriend, maybe. A nice, ordinary guy who worked hard and had good values. Dependable and decent. A man who would cherish her and look after her. No big car, no big money. No hotshot, no over-achiever. Definitely no high-roller.

But first she needed to get out of here.

She rubbed her teeth with her finger, smoothed and patted her hair, and readjusted the straps across her chest. She opened the door and took five steps across the dark cabaret floor.

Glasses were piled up at the corner of the bar, the gantry was lit from below, and the stark scent of booze and despair was all around. It seemed so rancid now, but she'd be the first to admit that she'd ignored the truth about Bruce running things in 'a certain way'. To him, everything and everyone was a commodity. Nobody and nothing mattered. There had to be more to life than rolling dice for a man like him.

She tiptoed past the door of the private casino, where he was waiting, and caught sight of her reflection in the mirrored doors. At least the dress had a designer label—she would be able to sell it in a heartbeat. And she would—as soon as she got to New York. It would make up for some of the back pay and pooled tips she was owed, because she sure wasn't going to get any of *that* now.

Ahead was the sunken black mat that declared its seedy welcome to Decker's Casino. She stepped on it and consciously ground the ball of her foot into his name. The automatic doors slid open and she slipped out and down the short flight of steps onto the street.

It had been a crisp, cold night when she'd entered and now it was a hot, clear day. She held a hand up to shield her eyes and felt sunbeams dance on her skin. The sensation of heat warmed more than just her bare arms—being out in the air, in the light, felt… *free.* But she wasn't dumb enough to imagine she was anywhere close to being in the clear. Not with no job and a twenty grand debt to pay off, courtesy of one Marilyn Jane Jackson—her mother.

She couldn't criticise her—not in a million years. Her mother was proud. She'd never ask for help. And Stacey knew all she'd have been trying to do was put on a show for 'those mean-mouthed gossips'. New curtains and new clothes. Stacey knew exactly where all those crazy ideas had come from. With no man in her life her mother had lost sight of the important things. She didn't judge her. God knew there were enough judges sitting on their porches in Montauk.

'Hey, where do you think you're going?'

Damn, her five-minute window of opportunity was closed. She glanced back and there was Bruce himself, like a raging pink-faced bull, standing at the top of the steps.

She spun round.

'Get back here now—you've got to earn that dress.'

Despite all her big talk, Stacey felt her heart thunder. Bruce was a scary guy, and no one ever spoke back to him—least of all a woman. She'd given him both barrels in front of everybody before she'd run off to the bathroom. Staff. Customers. His horrible henchmen. No, this was not good at all.

She didn't need to look to know that he had started down the steps. The pedestrian light flashed its *Don't Walk* warning, but what else could she do?

She ran.

Horns sounded and cries went up. Her heel caught in the black jersey of the gown. Fleetingly she wondered how much she'd lose off the resale value, but then the gleaming black hood of a limousine seared her vision and the sense of impact crashed like cymbals in her mind.

Her thigh… Her knee… But miraculously as she

slid down to the ground nothing else seemed to have been hit. She stumbled forward through more horns and cries and lines of cars revving and moving, and only then did she see the man.

From the limo's driver's door, emerging to stand tall and dark and incredibly like sweet salvation, a figure appeared and moved two paces into her path.

'Here,' was all he said.

And all she did was step forward and into his arms. There was no alternative. Some primeval part of her brain told her so.

She was aware of the cars, and she was aware of Bruce, but she was most aware of warmth and strength, of the opening of a car door and the sensation of leather, before all noise was extinguished and the door closed, sealing her in.

'Drive,' she breathed. 'Please.'

'The least I can do,' the guy said, and he put his foot to the floor. She felt a wrench as the force of acceleration pulled her back. She let out a gasp and automatically grabbed the seat belt.

'It's okay. You're safe with me,' he said, looking round at her as he put more distance between them and Decker's.

I'm safe with no man, she thought to herself, but she said nothing, only stared out of the passenger window at the blurry urban scenery. Her mind ran with possibilities—maybe Bruce had taken the car's registration. If he had it was only a matter of time before some dirty cop was blackmailed into reveal-

ing its owner. No matter how much this guy thought
he was leaving them behind, Bruce wouldn't be that
easy to shake off.

'All right?' he asked.

Stacey tried to calm her mind and shifted her
gaze from the passing neon outside to the dust-free
rows of knobs and dials inside. Now that she'd left
Bruce on the pavement she had to make some decisions—and fast.

She glanced at the guy's hand, resting easily on
the steering wheel. His skin was the caramel colour
of winter in Barbados. The fabric of his suit was the
dark silk of merchant banks and private members'
clubs. And his scent was pure unadulterated *Fortune 500*.

She sat up a little in her seat, twisted her neck—
which hurt—and tried to catch a few more details.
It had been a long time since she'd been this close
to this kind of wealth, but she'd been around money
growing up, so she could grade men in order of the
zeros in their bank account at thirty paces. This one
had zeros galore. She'd bet he was thoroughbred—
townhouse in Manhattan, ranch in Montana, villa
in Barbados.

That didn't faze her. Give her dirt-poor and decent
any day of the week. Some people seemed to think
money was their passport to be downright mean.
She felt her hackles rise at the memory and twisted
round further to get a better look, but the pain in her
neck caused her to flinch.

'It's okay. Try to relax. I'm taking you to hospital—to get checked out.'

Stacey stared out of the window anxiously. She didn't have the money for medical bills and, whatever people might say about her, she wouldn't take a dime she wasn't owed from *anybody*.

'I don't think so,' she said. 'Just drop me at the bus station.'

'Sure. But first you'll be checked out. I'm taking you to St Bart's. I'll have you looked over by my physician. Once you've got the all-clear I'll drop you off. Wherever.'

Stacey squeezed her eyes shut and shook her head. Why did men always think they knew best?

'Seriously, I don't want to go to any hospital. I don't need a bunch of X-rays.'

'You don't know *what* you need, Stacey Jackson. You never did.'

She jolted as if she'd been hit by the car all over again. She turned to face the guy. One of his eyebrows had shot up in a way she knew so well. And then it all fell into place. Her heart pulsed right up into her throat.

As if she were watching an old reel of film, Stacey looked on helplessly as scene after scene of sunshine, pleasure and then hard, dark pain flashed through her mind. Marco Borsatto. The boy from the right side of the tracks. The boy she'd fallen helplessly in love with. The boy she'd thought had fallen helplessly in love with her.

Silly, trusting little fool that she'd been.

'Marco. Well. Wow. What a small world.'

Her eyes widened now—she was back in the present. She tried to shift in her seat, away from him, but all she could feel was the jarring handle of the door and the pain that now seared through her body.

'Indeed,' he replied, turning back to the traffic as the Atlantic City scenery passed by in a blur. 'I wasn't sure it was you at first. But with a dramatic entrance like that—who else could it be?'

'Dramatic?'

He raised that brow and slanted her a glance.

'Dramatic,' he said emphatically.

'I guess you're right,' she said. 'I was never much good at playing the shrinking violet.'

She looked at his profile as he chuckled. *Wow.* He looked better than she remembered. And he'd been the hottest guy ever back then.

Marco Borsatto. What could she say? How ironic that the last time she'd seen him had been the first time she'd staged one of her great escapes. The very reason she'd staged it. The day that the tear in her heart had become a gaping hole of hurt. Marco had been her one source of strength. The one person in that town of gossips and snobs she'd trusted. And he'd ended up being the one who drove her away.

'So, apart from running dramatically into traffic, is it safe to say that life's been good to you? You look—well...'

He tilted her another glance that took in the whole

show. She looked down to see that the dress which had started out as barely decent was now bordering on the barely legal. She squirmed, and this time when she looked up his eyebrow had shot up again and his lip was distinctly curled.

'Life's been all right—thanks. I get by,' she said, tugging the dress back into place as best she could.

'You could have stopped the traffic even without throwing yourself at it. Good job the lights were just changing.'

'I don't normally dress like this—I was leaving work,' she added defensively, but her words were muffled in a gasp of pain as the car hit a pothole.

'No need to explain yourself to me,' he said quickly. His voice was calm—and all that quiet control that she remembered was now laced with deep overtones of firm command.

'And don't worry—I'll take care of anything that needs taking care of.'

Let me take care of you.

Stacey turned quickly to the window. The jolt of memory jarred like whiplash. Marco had been so kind to her once. He'd said those words. But she'd taken the kindness he'd offered and thrown it back in his face. Because girls like Stacey didn't mix with the Marcos of this world. She wasn't dumb enough to believe in fairy tales. In her world handsome princes disappeared, or turned into lazy, abusive, beer-swilling toads.

'How long has it been?' she asked. 'You were—what?—nineteen last time I saw you in Montauk?'

'Yes. Nineteen. Just before I hit the road. And you—you were still in high school?'

'Yes, I was sixteen. Thought I knew it all.'

She'd been sixteen. She'd been a mess. She'd come home that night to find that her mother had sold the car—their last remaining luxury. She'd been fired from her part-time job for using her mouth against a customer who'd insulted her, and she'd learned she'd been given the Tramp of the Year award by her classmates. Yeah, she'd been a mess, all right. So when Marco had caught up with her and asked her if the rumours were true she'd laughed in his face.

Of course they were true. Did he think he was special?

He'd turned his back on her and she'd done what any abandoned daughter would have done. She'd gone looking for Daddy.

'We all thought we knew it all,' Marco said. 'Comes with the territory. Refusing to listen and making the wrong choices. Isn't that what growing up is all about?'

She rolled her eyes, remembering.

'Are you talking about the night I left home?'

'Not especially. But I reckon it kind of fits the bill,' he said, smiling.

'Okay, so hitch-hiking wasn't my *best* plan—but how was I to know that my mother would mobilise everyone with a torch and a conscience. I was only gone three days.'

'I know. I was there. Torch. Conscience. Ticket to Rio burning a hole in my back pocket.'

Stacey cringed, remembering. It had been the worst weekend of her life. She'd bounced like a boomerang from one disaster to another. Her hare-brained scheme about finding her dad had spectacularly backfired and she'd come home with no money and absolutely no illusions that he was anything other than a sorry, selfish excuse for a man.

'Sorry I delayed your trip. But you made it to Rio in the end, right?'

He shook his head.

'Not that year—change of plan. But it didn't matter. I would have gone anywhere as long as it wasn't Montauk.'

Stacey nodded. She knew exactly what he meant.

'If I never see the End of the World, Long Island, again it'll be too soon,' she said.

They travelled for the next few minutes in silence, to the outskirts of town and the start of more exclusive addresses. Places where Marco would be right at home and where Bruce's name probably wouldn't cut it.

He turned the car into a lushly planted car park. A red cross and the words 'St Bartholomew's Medical Center' in deeply etched silver writing warned in hushed tones that this was the domain of the elite. Exclusively. The building itself was solid and secure, white stone, and for a moment a sense of calm descended. She felt it. She sat. Still. Silent.

'I don't think this will take too long. Then you can be on your way. But if there is any damage don't worry—I'll cover it.'

'Thanks,' she managed to say. 'Good of you.'

She reached for the handle.

'Stacey. A moment.'

She swallowed, then turned—carefully. He was sitting back in his seat, one elbow on the armrest, one hand on his knee. The picture of easy, moneyed charm. Like a warm, sunny welcome after the grim, gritty night. Sure and solid and secure. Exactly how she'd once felt in his company. Safe from the never-ending stream of her mother's suffocating worries.

Yes, he'd had it all back then—he'd even had a heart. Unlike most of his friends, she'd never thought him shallow. Or smug. Or arrogant. On the contrary. Somehow he'd made her feel—*valuable*. That she had as much to offer as any other human being. But it turned out that had all been in her imagination. Because at the end of the day as soon as he'd thought she was anything less than perfect he'd cast her aside faster than yesterday's trash.

She took a second—took him in. God, but he was handsome. He had lost all the soft traces of boyhood and taken on the harder mantle of manhood. His eyes, dark and deep, were fixed onto hers. She'd always had a thing for dark-eyed men, and now she remembered this was where it had all begun. But no one had the full package like Marco—eyelashes short and thick, and long, wide brows that framed his dark, enigmatic look so perfectly. The blue-black shading of his stubble perfectly outlined his mouth and the blunt cut of his jaw.

She couldn't draw her eyes away. The air in her lungs suddenly seemed to be completely lacking. His lips—those fabulous full lips that she remembered—parted. Then there was nothing but the shadow between them, the beat of her heart and the anticipation that rocketed all the way to throb between her legs.

'Marco...' she breathed.

He moved not a single muscle. There was just the flick of his eyes as they roamed across her face. He didn't reach across to grab her, didn't accidentally brush up against her leg—he even managed to keep his gaze above her jaw. He was completely and utterly impassive. And, worse, she felt that he was mocking her.

'Put my jacket round your shoulders before we go inside. You'll feel more comfortable.'

He opened the door and she hissed out the breath she'd been holding in. What a fool. *What a fool!* She had actually contemplated kissing him—*kissing* him! And—worse—she'd thought he was going to kiss her too. She must be out of her mind. After all this time? That bump had definitely gone to her head. She had to get her game on or she was going to let herself turn into a pile of mush.

And a woman with no home, no job and no money could not afford to be mushy.

Marco opened the door and stood there, ready to shield her with his jacket. She swung her legs out noting that the thigh-length split in the skirt of her dress was leaving even less to the imagination than the bodice. Another notch down in his estimation, no doubt. Ignoring the pain, she held on to the sides of the car and eased herself to her feet.

'Too kind,' she said, slipping her arms into the deep sleeves he held out and wrapping the navy silk jacket around her. He closed the door and clicked the remote key to lock it. Two beeps. One for every ten billion, she'd guess.

'It's not a problem,' he said, every inch the uninterested chaperone.

She felt the weight of his world envelop her in heavy fabric and wide shoulders. It was as if gold had been spun into the cloth and wishes might fall out of the sleeves. Life was not fair. Not at all.

'You've clearly done well for yourself, Marco. I think it was a beat-up farm truck I last saw you driving. Win a little on the slot machines?'

As soon as the words were out of her mouth she regretted them. His father had been a compulsive gambler. *Damn.* She scrunched her eyes closed, remembering.

'I don't gamble, Stacey—in fact I despise it.'

'I'm sorry.' It was all she could say, and she felt the thrust of his anger. 'I forgot.'

'I can't forget. We lost everything due to my father's gambling. *Everything.*'

She knew. It had been the very thing that had bound them together at one point—Marco's rapid fall from the elite ranks of Montauk society all the way down to the gutter. All the way, but not quite. He was a Borsatto after all.

'If I had my way I'd shut down every toxic casino in this town. And the others.'

'I'm glad not everybody sees it that way. I've made a living from them one way or another these past ten years.'

'You're entitled to your view,' he said, as if it was the most stupid thing he'd ever heard. Then he turned and began to walk towards the building.

She watched his retreating back, outlined against the white marble.

So what if he'd lost it all? She'd never had it in the first place.

She started after him, her heels dragging on the gravel of the car park.

'Not everyone who gambles is a loser, you know.' She fired the words into his back.

He paused. 'I guess not,' he said, turning slowly, judging her.

In the smallest slide of his eyes he was telling her that she had been found completely and utterly lacking. He stood there, framed in the white-pillared entrance. Sheets of black glass wrapped around the building behind him. Sunlight sparkled.

'But in my experience there are a hell of a lot more sinners than saints.'

'More whores than Madonnas? Is that what you're saying? Because I'm dressed like this?'

His mouth curved a little. He shook his head.

'I was talking about the customers, Stacey. Not the staff.'

There she went again—jumping to conclusions and shooting her mouth off like an unmanned artillery gun. She threw him her worst possible look but he didn't flinch.

'You told me you don't normally dress like that. So I assume it's your "uniform" if you were working today?'

Before she got a chance to answer an immaculately presented woman in a sleeveless tailored dress and heels, with the most perfect hair Stacey had ever seen, clicked across the marble entrance, hand extended, smiling her Ivy League best.

'Mr Borsatto, how pleasant to see you.'

'Thank you, Lydia, nice to see you too. I'm afraid I haven't got a scheduled appointment today, but I'd be obliged if you would arrange urgent scans for this lady.'

Stacey eyes flashed to the name badge which read 'Executive Administrator', whatever that was, even as the lovely Lydia arched her eyebrows then swept her with an all too familiar look. The one that said, *What's the likes of you doing with the likes of him?* That said, *You don't belong here.* The one that she'd

endured over and over in her youth. That always
ended with her losing her temper—because what
gave them the right?

But then she looked at Marco, and for a moment
she was right back in Montauk. Right back in the
little café where she'd worked and where 'the crowd'
had hung out. Where he'd keep his eyes on her in a
long, intense stare, telling her he had her back.

Back then.

'And we'll need the *best* possible St Bart's welcome, Lydia. Miss Jackson and I have had a minor
traffic accident, unfortunately. But she's kindly
agreed to get herself checked out. Just to reassure
me that she hasn't done any lasting damage.'

Was she imagining it? Or was there a warning
in those tones?

Whatever—the cold, calculating eyes of the other
woman told Stacey that it didn't make one blind bit
of difference what Marco said. They both knew that
she was a little plastic flower in his otherwise perfect garden. Here today, gone tomorrow. So don't go
getting any big ideas.

Stacey pulled Marco's jacket round her shoulders.
If the pink-faced, bull-headed Bruce Decker couldn't
get to her, there was no way on this earth that this
pristine princess was going to.

'Did you catch that, Lydia?' she said, stalking
right past her and slipping her a little of her best acid.
'The. Best. Possible. St Bart's. Welcome.'

CHAPTER TWO

STACEY LIFTED ANOTHER glossy magazine and began to flick the pages noisily. She took a sip of the pretty spectacular Italian coffee they'd served her and remembered again that money wasn't everything. But it sure could gild the world in a million beautiful ways.

This may be a hospital, she thought, *but it oozes more luxury than a five-star hotel.*

Even the scornful Lydia had been as good as instructed, and it was 'no trouble at all' to get Stacey everything Marco had asked for. And it seemed he had asked for everything. She'd been scanned and quizzed and prodded and now she was back in a private room, surrounded by all manner of things to eat or drink or read while she waited for some kind of decision.

She flicked on, through pages and pages of fashion, jewellery, homes and gossip. Exotic locations in European cities and tropical beaches. Jaw-droppingly handsome men and sombre-faced stick-thin women. Make-believe worlds that some people actually lived in.

People like Marco.

She looked up from the magazine to see he had stopped pacing for a moment and was sipping on a tiny espresso. Framed by two giant palms and some expressionist art, he was the very image of the self-made superhero. He could slide right onto the pages of this magazine and the world would sigh and drool and smile indulgently at how one man could have just *so much* going on.

He turned to put down the cup and walked out to take a call, and of course her eyes landed on the perfect male curve of his backside. His legs were clearly outlined in his trousers—strong and long. The man worked out. Of course he did. Back in the day he'd been an athlete and a team player. A hero and one of the crowd. Every single girl had wanted him to ask her out and every guy had wanted to be his buddy. The whole world had loved him.

And they still did. Including the crack team of nurses who kept zapping into her airspace like killer flies, patently ignoring Stacey while directing all their queries to him. It was as if he was some kind of deity, while she was completely invisible, or too stupid to know and understand what was happening to her. And it was sending that prickle of anger up her spine again.

'Where is Mr Borsatto?' asked Lydia, bustling in briskly for the third time.

'I don't know,' drawled Stacey, deliberately feigning interest in her magazine. 'Down the hallway doing some brain surgery?'

She ignored the tutting sound and continued to flick through the magazine. Everyone was getting on her nerves. The pain in her back had eased, but her head was pounding mercilessly and a purple bruise had begun to bloom along her thigh. That wasn't *their* fault—she knew that—and if she was hostile to them it was because they were the kind of people who judged a person by net worth. It didn't seem to matter what you brought to the table—it was all down to how much you had in the bank.

And pay-cheques didn't write themselves, she reminded herself grimly. Her cheques from Decker's were overdue and her fairy godmother was still AWOL. And this fabulous new job in New York City wasn't going to happen by magic.

She had to go and find it herself. She'd wasted too much time here already.

She swung herself round and tried to stand up. Pain shot up her spine and her head throbbed and pulsed. Nausea heaved in her stomach and she gripped her brow and closed her eyes. She hadn't slept in over eighteen hours and it was beginning to take its toll.

From the corridor came the unmistakably commanding voice of Marco. She could hear the dreaded word 'concussion' as the conversation moved itself towards her. That was the last thing she needed to know. She didn't have time for it. She had a life to get on with.

'Ready?' he said, appearing round the door, with not-a-hair-out-of-place Lydia beside him.

'Always,' she said, swallowing down some bile and trying to stand as still as possible so as not to hurt her head.

They continued their conversation, still ignoring her.

Her head continued to pound. She needed to get out of here...lie down. Go and die quietly somewhere she didn't need to listen to the vowels of the super-rich.

Marco picked up his jacket, still ignoring her. He held it out—an unasked-for modesty cloak in case her bare flesh offended any of the nice patients or staff in the hospital.

The prickle of anger became a surge that she couldn't ignore. She stepped away from the bed and stood as upright as she could.

'Hello! Over here! Anyone planning to tell me what's happening? Or is it the kind of news that's only shared with rich people?'

Marco turned to stare. He frowned, lowered the jacket.

'Your scans are clear. Everything's fine apart from the bruising.'

His eyes slid over her face, her neck and chest, and rested fleetingly on the slashes of fabric across her breasts. Just that, even now, still made her body pulse in anticipation.

'You're quite badly bruised.'

They both stared at her as if she was something the cat had dragged in. Dragged in to their state-of-

the-art uptown hospital. What did *they* care about
the person under the stupid dress? The working girl
who'd ended up here because she'd had enough of
being leered over and bullied? Who'd had enough
and made one of her trademark escapes—right into
the path of Mr Hotshot's limo?

'Yes, the bruises are from where I got hit on the
leg, Marco,' she said, and tugged at the thigh-length
split in her skirt to expose the red and blue bruises.
'By *you*.'

He stared. She bent her knee and twisted her leg
like the best showgirl Vegas could offer.

Lydia tutted and bustled off out of sight.

'Seen enough?' she asked, staring right into his
eyes.

'I've seen far too much,' he flashed right back.

'Yeah, but you never got to touch—did you,
Marco?'

'One of the few who didn't, Stacey. Let's not forget that.'

Only once before in her life had Stacey felt a
punch of pain so hard that tears had sprung and she
hadn't been able to hold them back. And it hadn't
been when her father had left and never come back. It
hadn't been when none of the girls had wanted to be
her roommate at summer camp. And it hadn't been
when she'd hitched her way to Philly, to her dad's
new house, to find that he had a new wife and a new
family and thought it would be better she didn't visit,
if it was all the same to her.

No, she'd managed to hold herself together each of those times. But then she'd returned from Philly and headed straight to the Meadows—longing to see Marco, longing to tell him she'd lied, that her anger had made her say those stupid things. Longing to tell him what she'd found out about her dad.

But Marco Borsatto had had his own troubles. That same day he'd been evicted. He'd had no time for a stupid girl who had caused the community such pain. That was when she'd first learned the true meaning of 'breakdown'.

Now, just like then, her throat burned, her eyes burned and her chin wobbled uncontrollably. Her hand flew to her mouth and she stepped back—once, then twice. He would *not* see her like this—nobody would. She spun on her heel, looked for the door. Getting away from Marco Borsatto for a second time became the most important thing in her life.

'No, you don't—not again.'

She saw his reflection in the glass and felt his hand slide round her waist. He grabbed her against his side and without losing stride walked her right out of the room, along the corridor and through the sliding doors.

Her bruised leg bumped against his, and her neck seared with pain as she tried to wrench away, but the more she pulled the closer he held her.

Two beeps and she was back in the car. Two seconds and she was being driven away.

'Make no mistake—I don't want to spend any

more time with you than you do with me. But for the next ten hours you're a high-risk concussion patient. And, much as I would rather leave you in the capable hands of the staff at St Bart's, I think they've had more than enough of your nonsense for one day.'

She said nothing. She saw nothing. A sob welled like lava in her chest. Her eyes burned like molten glass.

'So you'll come to my home for the night. You'll stay there until I know you're in the clear. And then you'll get a cab to wherever you want. You might not have any shred of a conscience, Stacey, but I'll be damned if I'll have you on mine a second time. Got that?'

'Consider yourself absolved,' she spat, but her burning throat, aching head and lack of sleep coupled with her whole collapsing world dumbed it down to one thick sob that she stifled with her fist. She wiped her eyes with the back of her hand and twisted herself to the side, so she didn't even have to breathe the same air as him.

'If it wasn't for your mother I'd put you in a cab to Montauk and send you back there. But she didn't deserve your selfish histrionics back then and she doesn't deserve them now. So let's say you and I agree to put up with one another until you've calmed down and I can safely pass back the burden of responsibility to her.'

'What are you talking about? The only person responsible for me is *me*.'

She felt the words but could barely say them—they wedged in her throat like hot bricks. Everything hurt…everything ached. But she kept her face to the side. She would not give him the satisfaction of seeing her so weak and vulnerable.

The car sped on.

Calls were placed and received.

He demanded and instructed and rattled off orders that made her head spin even more. A mechanic to check out his car, a pause on a half-dozen meetings, a bunch of flowers and a tennis bracelet to some woman whose shelf life had expired.

'Address?' he barked at one point.

She jumped but refused to look round.

'Give me your address, Stacey, and I'll get your stuff picked up. Unless you've got a better idea?'

Still she stared out of the window, the wonder of this whole unfolding drama making her feel more and more incredulous, more and more disorientated.

'Am I too rich to deserve basic manners from you? Is that it? Is it only poor people who are worth bothering about?'

'I can't believe that I *ever* bothered about *you*, that's for sure. I might have made a lot of mistakes back in the day, but thinking you were anything other than a giant egotistical hypocrite was the biggest.'

He barked out a laugh.

'Still at it, Stacey? Still opening that mouth and firing out your poison darts? You still think that'll fix all your problems, honey?'

'Don't "honey" me. I'm not your honey.'

'Ain't that the truth? You're no one's honey, are you? That would require you to be soft and sweet. You might look like butter wouldn't melt, but all you want to do is bite people's heads off. You know, I've been with you less than three hours and already I can feel my cortisol levels are sky-high. I live a pretty full-on life, and yet I haven't felt this much stress since the last time I saw you—ten years ago—do you know that?'

'Oh, I'm *so* sorry. I didn't realise *I* was responsible for your stress levels. How selfish of me! To bounce off your car and then insist that you drive me to your fancy hospital with all those super-friendly people who made me feel *so* at home. And then I beg you to make me stay overnight in your house while you threaten me with my *mother*! I am beyond inconsiderate.'

'This sarcasm is a new and even more unattractive trait.'

'Even more unattractive than I already am? *Wow.* I've hit pay-dirt!'

'Enough!'

He had stopped the car outside a huge pair of gates. He pulled on the brake so quickly that she slammed back in her seat. For a second they both froze, and in the startled moment that followed she thought she saw a flash of concern and an apology hovering at his mouth. But he shook his head and growled, unbuckled his seat belt and swivelled right round to face her.

'That's just about as much as I can bear to hear. What the hell's got into you? You know damn well that you were the most attractive girl I ever knew.'

Stacey stared, shocked. Marco's jaw was fixed and tense, his lips an angry line. His eyes blazed. In the still of the moment all she could hear were their breaths, shallow, panting, slightly out of synch.

He was so close now that she could see faint lines around his eyes—lines that had never been there before. Lines from laughter and sunshine that she had never shared with him. Lines from good times in faraway places with people she would never know. She'd made him laugh once. They'd had so much to laugh about back in Montauk.

There was no laughter now.

Tension. Tight across the breadth of his shoulders and in the thick column of his neck. She noticed now the full bloom of his masculinity—the man who had once been the boy. The boy she had once loved.

'You *are* a very attractive girl,' he added, his voice quieter now, a mere imprint of those deep, fierce tones. 'I don't know what's happened, Stacey. I thought your hard edges would have rubbed off by now. But seems like you've got more and more jagged and angry with the world.'

With each word his voice softened. Her defences began to crumble. She could take everything the world could throw at her when it was hostile. She could defend and attack in equal measure. She was a match for anyone—male or female—and she never, *ever* left anyone in any doubt as to how they measured up in her eyes.

But she could *not* take kindness. It undid her at the very foundations. All her strength was sapped away, like a finger pulled from the dam.

The tears finally sprang and tumbled one after another in hot, wet streams down her cheeks.

His eyes filled with concern.

'You're crying,' he said softly. 'Stacey, I'm sorry. I've never seen you cry.'

'Yes, I'm crying—and I never cry. I *never* cry!' she sobbed, furiously rubbing at her face and gulping back the sobs that threatened to choke her. 'I was fine—and now look at me. I don't need your help. I don't want you. I don't need anyone and I don't need you to contact my mom. She doesn't need to know any of this. It's fine. *I'm* fine.'

She rubbed and rubbed and gulped and sobbed and her nose began to burn. She searched in her little purse. But she didn't have a tissue—she was never that organised. She wasn't like her mother. Her poor mother who'd crumple if she thought anything had happened to her.

'I haven't contacted Marilyn. I wouldn't do that. I'm not *all* monster, you know. Here.'

She looked through the blurred shapes that were all her eyes could see and saw Marco offering her a pure white linen handkerchief.

'Take it,' he said when she turned away. 'For God's sake, it's only a piece of cloth. Come here, then.'

And he cupped her chin in his hand and began to dab her eyes and her cheeks. She smelt the spicy blend of his cologne and felt the gentle press of his fingers with every touch. She felt strength. She felt kindness. She couldn't bear it.

She pulled away.

'I hate you, Marco,' she sobbed into the linen square. She wiped her eyes and blew her nose. 'I hate you so much.'

He sat back. She could hear him laugh in between blowing her nose.

'Plenty do, sweetheart. Plenty do.'

'We both know that's a lie,' she said, giving her nose one final blow. 'Unless you've had a personality transplant in the last five minutes. Those nurses were all over you like a rash. It kind of made me want to hurl.'

He laughed again. It was the best medicine she could have wished for.

'Ah,' he said. 'And I thought it was from eating those pastries. You looked as if you hadn't seen food in days.'

He turned back to the road and nosed the car in through the double gates.

'No. Although that would be a great excuse,' she said, her voice still thick with tears and tiredness. 'They were amazing. And the coffee.'

She swallowed, shook her head.

'Thanks,' she said, cursing her own selfishness. 'Thanks for getting me checked out. I appreciate it.'

He parked the car in front of a villa—pillars, wide windows and a terracotta-tiled roof. Planters stuffed with flowers and miniature trees and topiary. A rich man's house. A *very* rich man's house.

She flipped down the visor to look in the mirror. Panda eyes—the eyeliner had completely melted and seeped into her eye sockets. She pressed with her knuckle to wipe away what she could. Even her nose was swollen and red. She'd never looked worse in her life.

'Forget it. The staff did it all. I'll pass on your thanks to Lydia and the team.'

Instantly she saw Lydia's perfect hair, Lydia's perfect face. She slammed the visor shut on her own disastrous image.

'If it's all the same I'll pass on my own thanks. To those that deserve it.'

'There you go again. Flying off in some crazy direction, damning people whose only crime is not coming from the same social class as you. You want to tone that down, Stacey, or it'll start to show on your face. And then you'll be left an angry and bitter old woman—all alone.'

With that he got out of the car, closed the door and walked towards his house.

She sat in silence, enveloped by his words as they settled all around her, harsh and hurtful. But the truth of them was clearer than a clarion call. She knew she didn't make friends easily. She knew she attracted men but just as quickly scared them away. She knew she was lonely to the bones of her being.

But she'd rather be lonely than patronised, or mocked, or judged.

Marco stopped, turned, raised a solemn eyebrow and held out his hand in a gesture of welcome. Or sufferance.

She didn't feel welcome. She felt backed into a corner by Marco's conscience.

What a guy. She could imagine the porch gossips already: *'You know he even looked after Stacey Jackson in his own house when her mother was out of town.'*

With the last of her strength she stifled the agony of her body and her head and her heart and swung herself out of the car. She could feel the cords of the town pulling tight round her neck. She could feel them pulling her back there, like fishermen landing their catch.

But nothing had made her more sure of her decision to have left the place than spending this time with Marco. She *hated* that world. She hated everything he stood for. And she was counting down the seconds until she could be back on the road, doing her thing, as far away from those parochial, judgemental pains in the ass as it was possible for her to be.

CHAPTER THREE

'Bedroom's at the end of the hall. Bath's en-suite. Terrace is accessed from every room.'

He tossed his keys down onto the gleaming work-top and watched them slide right into the fishbowl. It was empty. Had been since…always. Despite every girlfriend who had ever passed through having the notion that she was going to fill it up one day. Thank the Lord that had never happened. The last thing he needed was a goldfish as hostage to his so-called commitment phobia. On top of everything else.

What women didn't get, of course, was that he was the most committed guy he knew. Commitment was the reason he got out of bed in the morning. But it wasn't anything to do with pledging his troth to a woman—after the upbringing he'd had, pledging his troth was the last thing that was ever going to hap-pen. Why not just give his legal team a million-dollar retainer and cut straight to the divorce?

It baffled him. Completely.

No, commitment was all about getting things back

to the way they should be. And right now he was this close to getting it all back. *This close.*

Yes, only these next two days to get through and then he'd be back in Montauk, lounging in the Polo Club and watching Preston Chisholm slide the vellum deeds of Sant'Angelo's—the final part of the Borsatto estate—across the table for him to sign.

Ten long years he had waited for this moment. Ten years of being in hock to poverty, to shame, and worst of all to pity. He could handle almost everything, but the twisted compassion that some of the Montauk natives dished out amounted to nothing short of blackmail.

He reached for the coffee machine, thinking of the women who had held their breath, hoping that poverty would reduce him to becoming some sort of gigolo. Women who'd been so-called family friends. Young and old alike. And the men who'd relished watching Vito Borsatto's son lose every last cent, every brick, every blade of grass that the most influential family in the Hamptons had ever owned. Generations of Borsattos had built it up. And in one short year it had all gone.

That was when he'd truly known who his friends were. Finding out his father was a philandering compulsive gambler and his mother was a vain, narcissistic drunk hadn't given him a lot of cachet. He had watched them destroy themselves and then one another and had been able to tell no one. Because the shame had been almost the worst thing of all.

Watching as first the gangsters and then the banks had rolled in to take the estate in chunks. And then the biggest gangster of all: Chisholm Financial Management. Gangsters in three-thousand-dollar suits with fewer scruples than any of the rest. Standing in the dilapidated summerhouse that last day, when the devil himself, Mr Chisholm Senior, had arrived personally to evict him. The pleasure he'd taken in marching him off his own land—the last of the Borsattos. Mother and father long gone. Nothing left but dirt and dust.

Marco drained the last dregs in his cup and poured another.

'You get through a lot of coffee. Anybody ever tell you that?'

She'd been there that day. Stacey Jackson. She'd turned the town upside down with her attitude and her disappearance. And then she'd swanned back in as if nothing had happened. As if she'd expected some kind of welcome committee...

Was it any wonder he had a jaded view of women? They were after you for your money or your body. Your house or your head. All of them wanted a piece of something. He hadn't met a woman yet who hadn't let him down. Including his own mother. Women equalled trouble—especially this one.

'Maybe I could have one, if it's not too much trouble?'

He kept his back to her, pulled another cup from the cupboard and poured.

'Not at all,' he said, slowly turning to hand it to her. 'Sorry. Maybe I've been living on my own too long.'

She pulled out a chair and eased herself onto it, cradling the cup between her hands. And, dammit, he was drawn to her. Even though she should have her own 'Wanted' poster for crimes against humanity, there was something hugely seductive about her. It was all sex appeal, of course. Something in the way she wore his jacket. Something about how the shoulders dwarfed her and enveloped that body. Something that suggested ball-breaker Stacey was a vulnerable little girl underneath all that attitude. Despite what he knew about her.

'Living on your own? Oh, come on,' she said, taking a sip and watching him over the rim, those huge blue eyes underscored with the inky remnants of her tears. 'I bet you've been beating them off with a stick, Marco. A hottie like you.'

He looked at her—looked at the highlighting of her breasts in the shadow between his lapels.

'I can't say I've ever had to beat off a woman, no,' he said.

There was a very slight pause. A shared moment when he knew and she knew that there was another agenda at work between them. There had been back then and it was just as strong now.

She took another sip and put the cup down—slowly.

'Yeah, well,' she said. 'I'm not really interested in your bedroom antics.'

He nodded. 'Maybe we should clear that up now. So there's no doubt.' He held her gaze across the table.

'Meaning…?'

'Meaning that I didn't invite you here for anything other than a place to stay until you're in the clear. It's my duty—I'm responsible for your accident.'

Her eyes suddenly blazed.

'Are you suggesting that I'm trying to seduce you?'

'Stacey, would you get off your high horse for one goddamn moment? I'm not suggesting anything. I want you to know that while you're here I won't take advantage. That's all. We had a thing once, but we're both adults now and we can stay overnight in the same house without you worrying that I'm going to make a pass.'

She smirked her lopsided smile and hid behind the curtain of her hair in that way that she did.

She pushed her cup away. 'That's very noble of you, Marco. It hadn't crossed my mind that you might want to—to go back there, if I'm honest. But it's mature of you to make sure there are no misunderstandings.'

She chose that moment to ease the jacket from her shoulders and twist round to place it over the back of the chair. It might have been complete coincidence, but as she raised her arms his eyes slid all by themselves to the satiny gleam of her breasts, caught in the criss-cross of black fabric across the bodice of her dress. And of course his body reacted.

'You can count on it,' he said, still watching as she rearranged herself on the seat.

Then she looked pointedly at him and feigned a look of surprise.

'I'm sorry—have I spilled something?' she said, looking down at her chest. Then she took her time readjusting those goddamn straps over one breast and then the other, wriggling and jiggling her flesh and flicking at little flecks of invisible dust. It was a car crash. He couldn't look away. She was teasing him out of his mind. Just as she'd used to. Teasing but never giving out. At least not to him.

'So, how *is* your mother? Did she remarry?'

He lifted her cup and turned away to the coffee machine. A few minutes making coffee and talking about Montauk ought to do the trick.

'No, thankfully she made a lucky escape. But there are so many assholes in the world. I'm sure you know what I mean.'

He smiled and refilled her coffee cup, put it down in front of her, noting the way she shifted in her chair. She couldn't resist.

'She's still in Montauk, right?'

'Yes, still there. Same house. New curtains.'

He frowned. 'Sorry—what?'

'Doesn't matter. What about you?' she said, changing the subject with another forced smile. 'Is the old gang all back in touch now that you've got all that bullion to sell? Or buy? Or whatever it is you do nowadays?'

He nodded. 'Something like that.'

He could go into it—tell her about his years spent in penury following the humiliation of being tossed out on his ass, the journey south, then east, bumming across Europe, then India, until he landed his first break exporting gold. Then his time in Italy, picking up what he could about winemaking from his extended family. Finally thinking that there might be a way back home.

But—no. There would be nothing to gain in sharing any of that. He'd drawn a line.

He drained the last of his coffee. So much caffeine, so much adrenaline. So much stress...

Maybe he should go easy for the rest of the day. There was a lot still to do.

'So, been here long?'

She was looking round the kitchen, her eyes landing quickly on different things and then dancing on and moving back to his face. With that smirk.

'A while. A year.'

'Really?' She nodded contemplatively. 'Don't you hang out here much, then?'

'Not sure what you're getting at, Stacey...'

'Your villa. It's pretty vanilla—almost as sterile as that hospital. No offence. Just not how I remember the Meadows at all.'

He lifted the two cups and walked to the dishwasher.

The Meadows. It had been years since he had heard his home called that. It was the name the locals had given it and it harked back to the first white settlers who'd come from England. But it had been Sant'Angelo's since the Borsattos had taken up residence there. And it would be Sant'Angelo's again soon.

'None taken. As I said—the spare bedroom is down the hall.'

She took the hint and stood up.

'I'm sure I'll find it,' she replied. 'And, hey, thanks again for the jacket.'

She patted it and—*dammit*—his eyes landed there again.

'And the trip to the hospital. I—appreciate it.'

She smiled softly and for the first time it looked genuine.

'As I said...least I could do.'

She nodded and picked up her purse, then started to make her way down the hallway. Her long brown hair sank down over the nape of her neck in a silken sweep, landing an inch above where the straps of the dress slashed across her back and a good six inches above where her perfect backside sashayed. He found himself watching, mesmerised. Hypnotised. It was as flawless as he remembered.

As a kid, every single thing about Stacey Jackson had caused some kind of chain reaction in him from brain to body. The way she'd walked into a room, the way she'd swung her eyes round to look at people, or more often to ignore them completely. The way she'd give nothing away to the world, but had somehow made people feel as if they knew all about her and wanted to know more.

Thank the Lord he was immune to everything now—apart from the primordial reaction in his brain telling him he still found her attractive. He was a man...she was made the way she was. It was just a mental process firing off. So she still made him hard? So what. It didn't mean he had to act on it.

She was halfway down the hall now—taking her time, taking up *his* time.

She stopped. The prints on the wall there were huge, brightly coloured inks that represented the Southern Hemisphere sky that he'd stared up at for all those months on the road. Months when all he'd had was his health and his will to survive.

Stacey swung her head over her shoulder and eyed him with that profile that packed as much punch as any Hollywood starlet.

'Now, *these* are interesting,' she said. She stared at the prints, moved her head this way and that. Made a little face. Cut him a glance. 'Original. A little more flavoursome.' She licked her lips.

He looked away. Anything but be faced by the curve of almost completely bare breast that he could now see so clearly as she lifted her arm up to touch the frame. He had to get her the hell out of his sight.

'Thanks. We'll eat at seven. I suggest you shower and make a few calls. Or walk about quietly. Or something. And do me a favour—don't lie down and fall asleep. I don't want to add to the drama.'

She opened her mouth to give him another smart remark but he put his hand up, turned his head to the side.

'And another favour? Get some damn clothes on. It's three in the afternoon, for God's sake. The time for putting it all out on display is well past.'

Her face, already tense and tearstained, turned away. Silence fell around the bitter words he'd just thrown. From the glass roof above daylight flooded in, landing around her outline for all the world as if she was an angel in a chapel.

A woman less like an angel he had never met, but in that moment he felt angry—with himself. And as she stood there, regarding him, she almost looked ephemeral. It stopped him dead in his thoughts. Stacey Jackson was the one who'd got away. She was the one who'd shaped his view of women for ever. She was both his adolescent fantasy and the rock it had perished on. And he was damned if he would fall under her spell again.

He took the few steps up the corridor past her, shaking his head.

'I'm going to be busy for the next hour or so. Just try—try not to get into any trouble. Okay?'

He made it to his study, shut the door and breathed.

Three paces across the room and he turned on the huge monitor. Instantly his emails appeared. He scanned them, looking for the one he knew was on its way. And there it was. From the realtor representing Chisholm Financial Management.

Marco leaned down on the desk and grabbed at the mouse, sliding it quickly to bring it to life. He clicked on it. Words appeared.

The door sounded across the hall. Good—she was inside, out of sight and out of mind. He skimmed the email. Yep, the offer had been acknowledged. And everything was in order. It was all coming together perfectly.

There was the sound of the shower starting up. Great. That would keep her busy for a while. Give him time to fully digest this. Adrenaline was flooding his body. He was closer than he'd ever thought possible.

Instantly his mood lifted. Instantly he could see blue skies again. He'd been coiled like a spring all day. And there had been no need. Preston Chisholm Junior was going to deliver it all back—just as his father had taken it all away.

Well, well, well. Preston Chisholm. How life turned around. It seemed like only yesterday that he'd been sitting opposite to him in Betty's, watching him as he watched Stacey wait on tables. The look in his eyes had been predatory. A look that had wound up with him landing a punch on the guy.

Nobody had liked Preston Chisholm back then. And fewer liked him now. Still, as CEO of the bank that both bankrolled and mortgaged half the properties in town, people were cautious in showing it.

Not someone like Stacey, though. She'd still give

it to him both barrels. Just like that day when she'd found out that he'd punched Preston because of what he'd said about her. She'd been furious. The same afternoon Preston had practically salivated all over his polo shirt, he'd dragged him by its pristine collar out back and sunk his fist into his stomach.

A great noise had gone up, raising the dust in the car park, and then out had come Stacey in that little yellow dress and white apron the girls wore at Betty's. Preston had been curled up like a shrimp, bawling like a baby. He had been standing over his handiwork and Stacey had completely overreacted.

Who did he think he was? She could defend her own name, thank you very much. He could mind his own business or go and play the hero for someone else.

Marco smiled at the memory. For about the tenth time today. For all she'd made his stress levels rocket, she'd made him laugh too. All that personality in one perfect package.

He listened to the noises she was making across the hallway. Normally he hated the intrusion of a woman in his home. God knew he'd tried, but he couldn't get used to it. Moving his stuff, asking for closet space, filling the air with nonsensical chatter. The first day it was fine. It was okay. After a week he'd be finding problems with his offshore businesses that he had to solve personally. After two weeks he'd quit making excuses and get the jewellers on speed dial.

Was he going insane, or was he smiling at the cute little noises Stacey was making?

He might be smiling now, but five seconds together and their sparks would be flying right into a fireworks display that could light up the entire eastern seaboard.

What a *Fortune 500* per cent bore Marco had turned out to be, thought Stacey as she wound her hair in a towel and rubbed some fancy cream into her puffy pink face. She would never have pegged him as vanilla, but that was the only flavour she could scent from him now. His safe suit, his 'right' car, his hair trimmed just along his shirt collar line. He probably used shoe trees.

She stepped into the guest bedroom and looked around. Pale walls, wood floors, dark rugs. She'd choke to death in a place like this. It was as sterile as St Bart's. Nothing with any character except for the prints in the hallway. And her outrageous dress draped across the bed.

She could hardly put that back on.

Not after his strict instruction to cover up.

She wasn't imagining the chemistry—was she? He *was* looking. She'd caught him looking a thousand times. But he sure wasn't acting on it. That was the biggest change of all. He'd never let his class or his money guide his actions before. He'd played it straight down the line. He'd even played it *over* the line. Defending her honour from the creepy Preston

Chisholm. She'd laid into Marco for sticking his nose in, but secretly she'd loved it. He'd been ridiculously overprotective—right in front of the whole crowd. And she'd relished their shock and awe at their poster boy being gallant for white trash Stacey.

But he was playing with a different deck now. He couldn't have been clearer that he was finding her a turn-off rather than a turn-on. But she was smarter than that. It wasn't about biology—it was all about class. Turned out he was exactly the same as the Montauk snobs after all.

She couldn't wait to get out of here and away from every memory of that place.

Meantime she'd better find something to wear.

She started to look in the drawers, pulling each one open and rifling through them. Shirts in shiny cellophane wrapping paper. White vests in boxes. Black socks in little unworn balls. Coils and coils of leather belts in various shades of boring brown.

An old college baseball shirt.

She pulled it out and put it on, then slammed the drawers closed and sat cross-legged on the floor, staring at herself in the mirror. French doors opened off to her left and the day was as beautiful as it had been when it started. She stood up, yanked the towel from her hair and ran her fingers through it. It would dry in big waves unless she got at it.

Maybe she should go and ask him for a hairdryer.

She looked in the mirror again—bare legs covered by a ribbon of shirt. Maybe she shouldn't…

She pulled open the French doors instead and went out onto the terrace. The sun was glorious on her pale skin, but she would burn in a heartbeat if she stayed out in it. She looked along the white-walled, clean-tiled terrace. Regulation ferns in regulation terracotta pots. She'd bet there was a regulation pool round the corner. Probably usually had the regulation blonde in it too.

She walked along, her feet slapping on the marble a little too forcefully. But spite did that. Spite got you by the throat and choked all the fun out of your day. Left you sitting in your own little pool of misery. But sometimes it was worth it. Sometimes it felt better to lie in the sewer than to be constantly fighting your way out of it.

Stacey turned the corner and prepared herself for an image of Marco—maybe with his shirtsleeves rolled up daringly past his wrists, his hands free, sipping water or dictating a memo to *buy, buy, buy* or *sell, sell, sell*. Or to order more leather belts in a shade of sludge—no, make that mud.

But he wasn't there.

He was standing in his office watching her through the one-way glass. What the hell was she wearing now? How was it possible that his ugly old college shirt could make her look even more appealing than the full-on 'do me' dress she'd been wearing?

He downed the double espresso he knew he shouldn't be drinking in one gulp and it burned his throat. *Good.* Pain. Maybe if he sat with his hand in the fire he could cause blisters in his brain and finally get that damned woman out of his head.

He hadn't even trusted himself to send an email back to Chisholm. He'd composed it, deleted it and repeated that action three times before he'd finally pressed 'send'. He'd paced the room and checked the markets. He could probably launch himself into space with the adrenaline coursing through his bloodstream.

He checked his watch. Three hours until seven. He could probably make her to go to bed at nine. And if he checked in on her at midnight then she'd be up and away at six or seven. He'd make her a decent breakfast. He'd run her to the bus station or wherever she wanted to go—within reason. And he supposed he should be arranging to get her things collected now. Surely she would have other clothes that were a bit more—ordinary.

He walked to the kitchen for another coffee, reached for a cup and pulled out two. He'd take her a coffee and get her to tell him the address.

He went back to her room and knocked. Nothing. Maybe she was still out on the terrace. He moved through with the cups and out onto the bright wide stones. No sign. He walked round the corner to the pool. Nothing. He walked to the ledge and looked over onto the sheer drop to the road below.

Where the hell *was* she?

And then he saw her—she'd dragged a lounger

right into the shadiest corner and was lying on it. Her head was turned to the side, her hair hanging over her face, eyes closed in sleep. Her legs were satiny pale and bare. She wore his shirt and one arm dangled loose, pink fingernails trailing on the ground.

'Didn't I tell you not to lie down?' he hissed to himself as he walked towards her. 'Stacey, get up— wake up!'

He walked towards her.

'Stacey!'

He put the coffee cups down on the ground. The liquid splashed his hand. He said her name and bent over her. He scooped his hands under her shoulders and heaved her up. Her head lolled back.

'Stacey!' he said.

'Hmm...?' she croaked out.

Emotions rolled through his mind...lust rolled through his body.

He looked at that sweet, beautiful face. Her eyes were heavy with sleep, lids half closed. Her mouth was moist and open, her cheeks flushed with the heat of the sun and her hair was in a tumble all around her face. She was soft and warm and she needed so much protection.

'Stacey,' he said again, pulling her closer.

And this time her eyes flickered.

'Marco?' she whispered.

He jerked back, still holding her, and watched as her half-glazed eyes fluttered open. She stared at him, then pulled out of his grasp, leaned back on her elbows.

He stood up. Stepped away. Ran his hand through his hair.

'Are you okay? I thought you'd—you know...'

She sat up on the lounger—feet on the floor, elbows on her knees—and leaned her head down. She moaned.

'Are you all right?'

'I'm fine. I'm—my head hurts.'

'Let me get you some water. Wait there.'

He raced back to the kitchen. What the hell had just happened? He'd wanted to kiss her. He nearly had kissed her! That was not supposed to happen. He'd made a conscious decision not to go there. His conscious decisions were what he lived by—they were irrefutable acts of will that he never, ever deviated from.

He poured water and took it back to where she still sat with her head in her hands.

'I'm calling a paramedic. I want to get you checked out again. You weren't supposed to sleep.'

'I'll be fine. Just give me a minute.'

She sat with her head bowed. He reached into his pocket for his phone. It rang before he'd even pressed a digit.

The name on the screen flashed up.

Preston Chisholm.

Financier. Owner of Sant'Angelo's. Keeper of dreams. All-round piece of trash.

'Borsatto,' he said, his mind whirring with where this might be going.

'Marco! I got your offer. Can't say it came as much of a surprise.' His voice was lazy. Patronising.

'Hey. I'm glad you called. How are you?'

'I'm happy to talk. But I think a deal like this should be dealt with in person. Since we go so far back I owe it to you. It would have to be tomorrow morning. First thing. In Montauk. Short notice, I know, but it's the only window I have for—oh, weeks now.'

Every bit of Marco's body tensed. There was no way Chisholm was going to weasel out of this deal. He wanted to meet face to face? Nothing would stop him. *Nothing.*

'Absolutely fine. I have a suite at the Polo Club. We can breakfast at eight.'

'I'll see you then.'

He clicked off the call and stood holding his phone like a grenade. The offer had barely been acknowledged. Legal should be all over it. What was Chisholm playing at? He couldn't have called this wrong, could he? Chisholm had no axe to grind—no need to play games. This was purely a financial deal to him. The emotion…? That was all Marco's.

'I've got to go.'

He spun round.

Stacey. She was standing up, looking awful.

Damn, he had this to take care of first.

'What are you talking about? You can't go any-where until you've got your things.'

'Look—you've got stuff to do... I've got stuff to do.' Her words were as sharp as ever but her voice was woozy when she spoke. 'Just give me my dress and I'll get going.'

This was all he needed.

'No. Not yet. I'll work it out. I've got to change my plans—I've got to be on the road early, but there's no question of you not staying with me tonight. It's just a matter of logistics. I've got a meeting I can't miss in Montauk. That's all.'

'Yeah, I heard.'

She lifted the water to her lips, sipped at it and then passed it back to him.

'I'd have thought you were done with that place.'

Done with that place? He'd never be done with it. Not until things were back the way they were sup-posed to be.

'Thanks for—everything. I appreciate it. But now I'd appreciate if you'd turn off the electric fence and call me a cab. Like I said, I've got...stuff to do.'

'What stuff?' he asked, only half listening. He was thinking about Preston. He was thinking about the house. He was thinking about all that he'd had and all that he'd lost. He was remembering the day they'd carried him out and imagining the day he'd walk back in.

And it was close now—*so* close.

'Oh, just stuff...'

Marco turned.

Stacey smiled.

Then she shook her head, as if to say, *Never mind* and he watched as her knees buckled, her head sank and she dropped to the ground like a stone.

CHAPTER FOUR

SENSATIONS OF SWIMMING in a dense current, floating up and then down, darkness and deep, heavy dreams. Being lifted. Laid.

Stacey came to in bed, Marco right beside her. She heard his voice first, urgent. He was saying her name. She was shaking, being shaken. She opened her eyes and saw his face.

'Honey,' he said, sitting back. He stroked her cheek with his knuckles. 'You gave me such a fright, but it's okay. The paramedics are on their way.'

She closed her eyes again as images began to sharpen in her mind. What had happened? She'd been trying to leave. Marco had been on the phone—talking about going back to Montauk, taking her with him. She'd wanted to get to New York, not Montauk. She still hadn't been to her apartment. She had no money, no job. Debts and worries had appeared like sinkholes in the road ahead of her.

She opened her eyes fully and the light pierced right into her brain. She put her hand up and twisted away. Marco had gone. There were noises in the hallway. In came people in green, with strong arms and cheerful faces. *Eugh*. She turned her head away.

'Hey, there, Stacey. You've had a bit of a fall. What day is it?'

'It's the day before the loan payment is due.'

There was a pause. Then Marco's voice.

'Stacey, answer the question.'

She kept her eyes closed.

'It's Wednesday. The payment's due Thursday.'

'How many fingers am I holding up?'

'Is that a serious question?' She sniggered into the pillow.

'She can be like this,' she heard him say. 'She doesn't mean anything by it.'

She twisted her head round, screwed up her face, held her hand up to shield her eyes from the light.

'Would you stop talking about me as if I'm not here? He's holding up three fingers. Okay?'

'She seems okay. We'll give her a check-over, but I'd say it's just been the heat and the shock—as you said.'

They were still talking over her head. She screwed her hands into fists and lay back on the pillow, eyes scrunched closed.

But there was no point in being awkward with the medics. She let them check her vitals and answered their questions and waited as patiently as she could for them to go so she could get up on her feet and on with her life.

'Stacey, take a look at these and pick out anything you'd like.'

Ten seconds after the medics had left she put down the glass of water, which was as much as her nauseated stomach would allow, and stared curiously at the next double act to enter the room—two of the best-groomed young men she had ever seen, pushing rails of neatly ordered clothes. They stood before her and eyed her like co-conspirators.

'What's going on?' she asked.

'You've been given *carte blanche*, girlfriend,' said one of them with a wink. 'A new wardrobe with clothes for every occasion. Nothing cut to the nipple or the ass is our only instruction so maybe it's easier to tell us what you *don't* want.'

'What occasion? What are you talking about?'

She lay back down on the pillow to the sound of chuckles. The painkillers were working. Everything was woozy. She longed to sleep.

'The lady needs a dress for dinner. Let's see what you got.'

Marco. Back in the room. She opened her eyes. She tried to sit up. The boys were holding up two dresses—one blue, one green. He was weighing each one up. They were preening like peacocks.

'Am I losing my mind? I do not want any man to choose me a dress. Look at what happened the last time!'

She flung back the sheet and swung out her legs. The bruise on her thigh was darker and the pain in her head sharpened to a piercing throb right across her temples. But she stood. She was done with lying down to this.

Marco eyed her with one brow hitched.

'Thanks, guys. We'll take the lot.'

'Including the lingerie, sir?'

'The lot. I'll see you out.'

She folded her arms over her body and waited until Marco came back in the room. He was out of his suit and dressed in loose light jeans and a plain white tee.

'We need to talk.'

'Sure, let's talk—but I'd prefer if you were sitting down,' he said.

'You don't get to make any more decisions for me.'

'You've been making a great job of doing that yourself!'

'Right until the moment you mowed me down I was.'

'I see. Are you including the loan payment due tomorrow? And the fact that you're on the wrong side of a guy who tried to clear out your apartment? And who's saying that you owe him money. And a dress.'

Stacey blanched. 'How did you find all that out?'

'Getting information's cheap, Stacey. Getting out of trouble can be a little more difficult. But not impossible.'

'Yeah, well, I sort out my own trouble. And I'd prefer if you didn't go snooping about in my life.'

'You lost that right when your "friend" started snooping about in mine.'

She frowned. He was looking stern. Calm, but stern.

'Let's just say that I've sorted the matter and leave it at that.'

'Leave *what* at that? What are you talking about? What's happened? Tell me—I have a right to know, goddammit!'

'Okay,' he said, clearly swallowing down his exasperation. 'Sit.'

He picked up a club chair as if it was a silk cushion and placed it beside her. Then he put his hand on her back and eased her down into it—gently. He pulled another one over and sat opposite her, elbows on his knees.

'From the top. I made a call to find out your address and get your things picked up and I got back a little more information than I bargained for. So I dug a little deeper and learned of your debt. That's no big deal—lots of people owe money…more than you. But those people aren't working round the clock to pay it off the way you have been. And working for crooks.'

She swallowed. She'd had no choice. She had to make ends meet and she couldn't let her mother down. But it was nobody's business but hers. She'd told no one. So how did he know about the debt?

She stared at him.

'You called my mother, didn't you?'

He nodded. 'I had to. You'd been in an accident and you'd collapsed. She had a right to know as next of kin, if nothing else.'

Stacey wrung her hands.

'You called my *mother*. I've spent years trying to get her to stop worrying and you blow the whole thing wide open.'

She looked off to the side—couldn't look at that big, handsome face, the concern all over his eyes—without wanting to slap him.

'Your mother trusts me. And knowing you're in my care probably makes her less worried about you than she's been in years.'

Her anger pushed her to her feet.

'You called my mother!'

She could hardly believe her own ears. She operated strict filters on what her mother learned about her life. Everything was fine and nobody was anything other than adorable. The world was filled with candyfloss and cake. What possible reason was there for telling her the ugly truth? Hadn't she had enough of her own dramas to deal with for years?

Stacey looked at him. He had no idea what he'd done. 'What else did you do?'

Marco sat back in the chair, as if he was going to light a cigar and tell an interesting anecdote.

'I paid off your debt. I collected your wages. I packaged up your things. They're in the car, all ready to go.'

'Is there any area of my life that you *didn't* get your greasy fingers all over?'

He shrugged. Smirked.

'I have no information about your love-life. That remains your own guilty secret.'

She tossed her head back, felt a twinge in her neck. It didn't hurt. But the pain of him stamping all over her life was immeasurable.

'Of course. You're quite prepared to bulldoze your way through my career, my relationship with my mother, my health, my finances—but admitting an interest in my love-life? That would be a step too far, wouldn't it? Because that would take you into an area that's a little too close to home—where once upon a time you had an interest of your own. Until all that money began to get in the way.'

He frowned at her. 'Don't be stupid. You're not even making sense. I don't know anything about your love-life because it's not my business and I didn't ask.'

'Liar. It's because you're frightened of what you'd find out. You wanted me back then, Marco, and you still do. You just haven't got the balls to admit it.'

'I see what you're trying to do here, Stacey. You're just trying to cause another fight so I'll back off. But it won't work.'

'What I'm "trying to do"? All I've been "trying to do" since you ran me over was get the hell away from you. But everywhere I go, everything I do, you're all over it. Even down to the colour of my panties!'

She threw her arm out to the room to show him the twin rails of clothes and the boxes of lingerie that sat beside them. Marco didn't move. Merely sat there as if he was patiently waiting for a toddler to finish their tantrum.

'I can categorically guarantee that your love-life is your business alone. I want no part in it. But I *have* made an undertaking to see you safely to Montauk. Your mother is on her way back there. Or at least she will be in a few days. You didn't know she was in Toronto, did you? She met a guy online. He lives there.'

'Is there any end to this?' she asked, cradling her head in her hands. How dared he scour her life and her mother's life for facts she didn't even want to know herself?

'An end? You can work that out with your mother. My part is over in three days, when I make sure you are safely back home, and by that I mean your own home. The twenty grand—we can work something out. I'm not going to miss it anytime soon, if I can put it that way.'

'You can put it any way you want, but the truth is that you are bribing me.'

At that he rose to his feet. '*Bribing* you? You call acting responsibly, doing my duty, taking care of you bribing you?'

They were toe to toe now. She could see how pronounced his stubble was, she could smell his spicy scent, could *feel* his maleness.

'Yes. And I don't know what you think you're

getting out of it other than playing the hero the way you've done your whole life.'

'Is that right?' he said.

'Yes,' she hissed. 'Everyone's hero. Except mine.'

She stepped even closer. She felt stronger and stronger with every second. She felt blood returning to places that had been parched. She was invigorated, and she was not going to roll over and play ball just because of some deal that had been cooked up between Marco Borsatto and her *mother*.

'You think you'll ride back into town with another feather in your cap because you've got *me* in tow—beholden to you. Tamed. Is that what this is all about?'

'You're reading far too much into this, Stacey. This is a simple matter of following through on my duty to you after the accident and to your mother for being a good person.'

He was eyeballing her now. She eyeballed him back, then let her eyes drift to his mouth. His lips were slightly parted.

'You're so *amazing*, Marco. Always doing the right thing. Every time. Marco Borsatto. *What a guy!* But I remember the real you. I remember the bad boy you wanted to be.'

'Is that right?'

He was so close now she couldn't slip a breath between them without it being felt.

She saw his nostrils flare as his eyes dropped to her mouth. She saw the pulse in his neck, sure and strong. She saw dark chest hair peeping above the hooped collar of his white T-shirt and the cotton stretched across the firm muscles of his chest. She saw the veins on his biceps stand proud. She felt herself drawn to touch them.

'I'm the forbidden fruit, though, Marco. One bite of me and you'll lose it all.'

She flashed him her sultriest smile. And waited.

He reached forward—one hand. Breath died in her throat.

'One bite?'

He pushed his fingers through her hair, grabbed the back of her head and tugged her forward. He gently cupped her jaw, then ran his thumb over each lip, tugging her mouth to the side. He dragged his fingers over her cheeks, never lifting his eyes.

He caressed her neck, trailed his finger along her collarbone.

As if a river had burst its banks her body flooded with life. She pushed herself forward, longing for more of his touch, waiting.

He shook his head. 'Not hungry.'

He dropped his hand. A phone rang. She stood frozen in the moment. He pulled it from his pocket, flicked his eyes to the screen and answered it.

'Mrs Jackson. No, you're not disturbing anything. Yes, she's here. She's looking much better. Of course you can talk to her. Only don't keep her too long— we have to hit the road in an hour. See you Sunday.

Sure—take your time. It's no problem at all. Glad to help—you know that.'

He cocked her an eyebrow. She mouthed the worst curse she could think of. He smiled the biggest smile—all teeth and crinkled eyes. Then winked and passed her the phone.

'Stacey, it's your mom. She wants a word.'

She took the phone, drew her eyes from him and turned on her heel.

He watched as she walked away, feet slapping on the floor, her normally strident tones quiet and mellow. He heard her reassuring her mother over and over as she walked. He heard her telling her that it was nothing at all—a tiny bruise you could hardly see. That Marco was making a fuss and, yes, it *was* incredible that of all the cars in the whole of Atlantic City she should trip up next to his. Who'd have believed it?

He heard her say that he had a lovely house—just lovely. And that he had fitted it out *so* nicely. The curtains were beautiful and he had such a big, bright kitchen. She'd absolutely love it.

He heard her walk out onto the terrace, pausing every now and then to listen to another question and answering in the low and slow tones that even as a teenager she had used to soothe her mother's anxieties.

And as he listened he felt something slide into place inside him. Something that made Sant'Angelo's even more than an object of desire. Because he realised that it wasn't just the bricks and mortar he was fighting for—it was his whole childhood. It was Montauk. The Jacksons were Montauk-born-and-raised. They were its fields and its beaches, its harbour and its seas. They were *What can I give?* instead of *What can I take?* They were it. Heart and soul.

And if a town could produce even one more Stacey Jackson then it was a hell of a place.

CHAPTER FIVE

STACEY PULLED AT the seatbelt that was cleverly extending itself towards her and buckled it across her lap. She settled herself into the seat and stretched out her legs, looking down at the navy leather leggings and silk tunic she'd chosen to travel in. They were the last word in luxury—and the other items she'd packed in the luggage that Marco was now stashing in the boot were admittedly gorgeous too. Tasteful, elegant and totally unlike the dress that she'd been wearing the last time she'd sat in this seat, which should be winging its way to a charity shop with a clear health warning.

So she'd rolled over? She'd accepted his 'offer'? What else could she do under the circumstances? Her mother was beyond happy that she'd even 'bumped into' Marco, let alone was being chaperoned by him. She adored him! Like everyone else from End of the World, Long Island, she'd been in thrall to the town hero since—for ever.

Yes, he'd played the juiciest ace in the deck and she was powerless. For now.

She flicked down the visor and caught move-
ment—Marco, pacing back and forth behind the
car, phone to his ear, hand in the air. Such an Italian
gesture. That part of him he'd always tried to play
down. She'd never pressed him on it because she'd
always known how fiercely he guarded his privacy—
and that whatever it was that his father had done sat
heavy in his heart. But he couldn't stifle what was
in him. Directing, dominating, deciding.

Thinking he could make decisions for people
without so much as a *Mother, may I?* He didn't need
to ask for permission. A guy like him was so busy
doing 'the right thing', and everybody was so busy
fainting at his feet, that nobody noticed he wasn't
as sorted and happy as he made himself out to be.

He was deep. Grand Canyon deep. And there
were no signs in that house or anywhere else of any
woman softening him up.

Outside there was the sound of the boot being
closed.

He paced around and opened the driver's door,
slid his big frame inside, filling the air with that
sense of command. Certainty. There wasn't anything to worry about—he had it covered. He had
your back. Whether you wanted him to or not.

He turned to her.

'All set?'

He looked at her. Winked at her. He plugged the
key in the slot and grabbed the back of her headrest
while he reversed the car out onto the street.

'Sorry that took so long. I've got a couple of deals going down and I like to have all angles covered—no surprises.' He swung the car round. 'Hate surprises,' he added. 'But then you know that.'

He laughed a little as he put his foot to the floor and the car shot off along the empty highway. The sun was setting on a warm, clear day. Ahead the ocean rolled and dragged, and behind them the city limbered up for another night of parties and fun.

'Hungry?'

'Ravenous,' she answered, clearing her throat and working her face out from its frown.

'Great—let's say we head north-east. Be good to check out one of my new places—if you don't mind mixing some business with pleasure?'

He looked round, eyebrow raised.

'This is *pleasure*?' she said. 'For the record, I'm in no hurry to get back to Montauk. *At all*. Not sure if you got that particular memo.'

'I got one from your mom, saying you'd be a good little girl. Did she copy you into that?' he asked.

And the flash of teeth and the crinkled eyes and the irritating, outrageous *handsomeness* of the man made her frown loosen completely and her smile begin to show.

'Matter of fact I was the one who suggested she send it.'

'Good.' He nodded. 'Great to be on the same page at last.'

'Is that the page where you're in such a great mood because you're heading back to Montauk like the sheriff with his bounty? You know the whole town is just going to *love* that? I can see the headlines now.'

'I'm sure the town will make of it what it wants to. The last thing I worry about is what other people think. So, the place I have in mind,' he said, completely changing the subject, 'is Valentino's—a new fine dining restaurant. It's been set up in a winery I bought a few years back. I've heard great things about the chef they hired, but I've never eaten there. It might be something to take up as a franchise to Montauk—you know, when I buy back Sant'Angelo's.'

That was news.

'You're buying back the Meadows? *Wow*. Marco—that's great. I mean… I know how much the place meant to you.'

He nodded, stared straight ahead.

'Yeah. That's what the meeting tomorrow is for. Keep it under your hat for now. Deal's not set in stone yet.'

She got it. No wonder he was so focused on getting there.

'I see. Well. No wonder you're in a good mood. I really hope you pull it off.'

The car rolled on. The city's glow faded behind them as they turned inland.

'There's no alternative. That house has been in my

family for generations. It should never have been lost. But it was. Well—you know all about it.'

Stacey smoothed a crease from her leggings. She did know all about it, of course. She knew about his dad and his mom and their problems. She knew about the businesses going, the land going and finally the house itself. She knew because she'd been with him through the worst of it.

She'd been right by his side the night he'd got the news that his mother had left the ten-thousand-dollar-a-week rehab clinic and vanished off to New Mexico with some guy she'd met. The clinic that Marco had funded himself, with the last of his grandfather's inheritance. At least his father hadn't been around to hear the news. He'd checked out of town and checked out of life. Oh, yes—Marco had had it tough back then.

And then she'd added to the mess by letting him think she'd been fooling around.

'Marco,' she began, 'you know back then—'

But he put his hand up. 'I don't dwell on "back then", Stacey. I got away from "back then" as quickly as I could.'

She opened her mouth. 'But there's stuff that maybe we should talk about...'

'I don't see the point. What point is there in dragging up the past? It's passed. Gone.'

She swallowed. It was the biggest regret of her life. She had to get it out in the open—if only to exorcise the ghosts.

'That night, Marco—when you asked me if I'd…'

'Stacey—I don't want to go there. None of that matters now. Maybe it did at the time, but not now. We've both moved on. You're…where you are. And I'm not who I was back then. I was a stupid kid. Messed up.'

She rubbed again at the crease in the leather. Looked at his hands on the steering wheel—his easy grip. Looked at his thighs—muscled, splayed open. Every inch of him telegraphed calm possession. What would he care now if Stacey Jackson had slept around or not? It wasn't as if she'd fallen out of Decker's Casino wearing a nun's habit. She'd been cast as the town tramp the last time she'd seen him and she'd looked even worse when she'd landed on his hood. First looks could be deceiving—but twice?

'Getting Sant'Angelo's back is what it's all about for me now. Back from Chisholm Financial—bunch of sharks.'

The sudden edge to his voice made her turn sharply.

'Yeah. Maybe I do sound bitter. I am. About them. But, hey…'

He lifted his hand from the wheel and touched hers. Squeezed it, held her fingers in his warm, sure grip.

'We're not going to waste our breath on that. We're going to head into Valentino's and sink some oysters and some Chardonnay. Or whatever Chef Luigi has got on offer.'

He still sounded bitter. Just a trace. But now wasn't the time to set out all the twists and turns of their teenage relationship. She'd find another moment—maybe.

'I'm not the biggest fan of oysters.'

'Or shark,' he added, smiling as he let go of her hand and put his on the steering wheel again. 'Or any other kind of fish, as I recall. Bit of a drawback in the world's best fishing town, if you ask me. But then I'm biased. Okay, here we are—there should be *something* to suit you here.'

She looked at the huge sign that declared they were entering the Borsatto Estates Winery and Hotel and Valentino's Restaurant. The tyres crackled on the gravel drive as he nosed the car right up to the entrance. A valet appeared, held open the car door and beamed a smile as he helped her out.

In seconds Marco was at her side, his hand carefully in the small of her back, easing her forward. Doors opened before them and people almost bowed when they saw them. It felt—*welcoming.* It felt warm and lovely.

'What do you think?' he asked her as they were seated at the best table, screened by a semi-circular glass-beaded curtain, subtly lit and discreetly tucked away in a corner.

Stacey waited until the waiter had draped a linen napkin on her lap before she spoke. 'It's amazing, Marco. I mean, it must feel incredible that all this is yours.'

He brushed it off. 'I guess—but nothing compares to how it's going to feel after tomorrow. When I know I've got the deeds to the house. When I'm finally free of anything to do with Chisholm Financial.'

Stacey lifted a glass of ice-cold water to her mouth and sipped.

'Yeah, I can buy that. Is it still a family business? Don't tell me that weird kid Preston has anything to do with them?'

Marco raised an eyebrow and nodded.

'The very same. Weird kid all grown up. At least the old man is out of the picture. I don't know if I could have handled negotiating with him. Son of a bitch.'

Stacey watched as Marco put his own water glass down carefully. Too carefully. As if he'd rather hurl it through the air and smash it against the wall. He drew his fingers back and bunched them—not quite into a fist, but curled with tension nonetheless.

'Don't tell me all those years of therapy didn't crack *that* particular nut?'

Marco caught her attempt to lighten the tone and smiled absently.

'The only thing that will crack that nut is walking back through the doors of Sant'Angelo's knowing its mine. I'm way past imagining kicking old man's Chisholm's butt off my property—the way he did me. Though I've got to admit the thought of it kept me going for years.'

She got it. Saw it clearly now. Everybody needed their engine and this was his. She had launched herself out of there like a rocket and he was coming back like a homing pigeon. They were so completely different! It wasn't just their social backgrounds—they wanted totally different things from life. They would never have made it work.

She ought to accept that now. He clearly had. She'd outright accused him twice of being hot for her and he'd given her two outright denials. What more did she need—a sworn statement under oath?

So she'd been imagining his interest. She had to have been or he would have acted on it by now. Knowing that should make her feel better, she supposed. She could relax. She didn't need to play any games. But no matter how you dressed it up it was rejection, pure and simple. She wasn't used to it, and she'd be lying if she didn't admit that it kind of hurt.

She lifted her glass again and sipped.

'I'm going to check out the kitchen. Say hi to the new guy. You okay to wait here?' he asked.

'Of course,' she said, glad of a moment on her own.

She drank some more water and closed the menu, slid it away and looked around. The place was packed, though it was so elegantly and cleverly designed that the atmosphere was calm and quiet and hushed.

People were glancing at her enviously. And for the first time since she could remember she didn't scowl or turn away. She smiled back at them—at total strangers. Usually she stared through people, sometimes worse. But being here with Marco she felt a sense that everything was going to be all right falling over her. She'd forgotten what it was like not to have any battles to fight. And it was kind of nice.

Nothing like the way she'd felt working at Decker's. The tension she hadn't even realised she'd been feeling. Always waiting for Bruce to explode at somebody. Always on guard in case he tried to get fresh with her. Always on the lookout for some trouble to come her way.

Bruce. She clenched her eyes closed. Marco hadn't gone into detail with her about what had happened and she didn't want to know. It was enough to know that she had put all that behind her.

She had, hadn't she? She didn't need to go back to that kind of life. Once she got to Montauk she could regroup, take some time, find something that she actually *wanted* to do.

She could help her mom make things for the house, the way she'd used to. She was good at needlepoint. She was artistic, had a good eye. Maybe she could find some way to make a living doing that kind of work, instead of helping people gamble away all their money. Where was the honour in that?

Where was the honour in sitting here playing make-believe with Marco Borsatto? She wasn't his girlfriend. She wasn't even his friend. She was the concussed albatross hanging round his neck. As soon as he could offload her he would. Of course he

would. Job done. *Tick.* Another medal for his chest—
another jewel in his hero's crown.

She didn't really need to play this game. She could
think of better things to do than spend even five seconds in Montauk. Okay, so he'd promised her mom,
but as long as she turned up on Sunday she could get
out of the rest of the prison sentence, surely? It didn't
matter a damn that she was wearing Gucci—she still
had no job and she still had to service a twenty grand
debt. It didn't matter if it was the Bank of Borsatto
or the Bank of America at the end of the day.

She was fooling herself thinking this was any
more than some twisted version of Pass the Parcel.

Stacey stood, shoved herself back from the table
and lifted her purse. They weren't that far from Atlantic City. She could— She could…

She started walking, eyes fixed straight ahead on
the door. To her left a hostess was seating a couple,
to her right a sommelier proudly displayed a bottle
of wine to upturned, interested faces.

She took a left along the dark, wood panelled
corridor. Saw glass doors and the driveway beyond.
Once outside she could figure out her options. She
always did.

She reached out for the handle.

'What do you think you're doing?'

Marco. Low, commanding tones. She paused mid-
step.

'It's getting boring, honey.'

He was right at her back, his hand placed firmly

on her waist. His voice whispered lightly at her ear
as he tugged her back into the restaurant.

'About to make a run for it? What do I need to do
to keep you by my side? Do you want me to hand-
cuff you?'

'What I want you to do is let me get on with my
own life. I'm fine. I don't need a nursemaid.'

'I'm not your nursemaid. But I *am* responsible. I
thought that was clear—but maybe I'm not talking
your language.'

He came right up behind her, an inch from her
body. She felt his heat, his lips at her earlobe, his
breath on her neck. She swallowed—felt the fever
return.

He kept her walking—but not into the restaurant.
Body on body he moved them along the dark hallway. Ahead of them were double swing doors, the
bright lights and the crashes and cries of the kitchen.
Above them was the dark wooden swirl of a banis-
ter winding upstairs. A lone velvet chair marked the
edge of an alcove and there, with a tug that caught
the breath in her throat, he stopped. He pulled her
around, backed her up and braced his hands on the
wall around her. He stepped close and covered her
body with his. Every part of them touched. Legs,
chests, faces. Darts of pleasure ricocheted through
her. Desire clenched deep in her core. She burned
for him.

'Marco—please.'

He pushed closer.

'Everybody is bending over backwards to make sure you're okay. Running after you...worrying about you. And you can't even sit down and wait for two goddamn minutes without deciding things aren't good enough.'

She opened her mouth to explain.

He put his hand up to silence her.

'I'm all out of patience, Stacey. All out of words. But I know one way to keep you subdued, don't I?'

She stared into his eyes. Laid-back and easygoing had gone. The Marco in front of her right now was total dominant male. Ten years flashed back. How many times had he kissed her into submission? How many times had she longed for them to take that extra step? But he hadn't made the move. And she had never been so bold. But theirs had been the best chemistry she'd ever known. She ached to rekindle it now.

'Yes...' she whispered.

And with that he closed his mouth over hers. Fiercely, relentlessly, ruthlessly he kissed her. He opened her mouth as wide as he wanted and plundered it with his tongue. He ground himself into her and grabbed handfuls of her hair as he pressed her further back against the wall.

Stacey's throat closed over a gasp. She tugged at his head, threaded her fingers through his hair and took her fill. She kissed his mouth, his cheeks, his brow. Her face was wet with his mouth and she couldn't stop it. That ten-year tide had swelled up and all she could do was go with the flow.

He grabbed her leg and heaved it round his waist as he ground deeper against her.

'You go nowhere unless *I* tell you.'

She clung to his shirt, bit at his lip. Her leg slid down and he grabbed it back up, held it with one hand. His other hand moved from her jaw to her breast.

'Understand?' he growled, squeezing it and moulding it.

She gloried in the sensations, the waves of pleasure that coursed and rolled through her body. *More*—she wanted more. She wanted to pleasure him as much as he pleasured her.

She knew how to enflame him even more. She looked him dead in the eye. 'Nobody orders me around. Not even *you*, Marco Borsatto.'

He pulled her other leg round him, scooped his arms behind her shoulders and worked her body so that her most sensitive area was pressed right against him. She threw her head back into the cradle of his hand.

'Is that right?' he asked, kissing her cheeks, her ear, her neck.

She rubbed herself against him. He thumbed her nipples. She looked down to where they had hardened to buds through the silk of her tunic. She looked into his face—flushed and wide-eyed and determined.

'Yes,' she breathed. 'That's right. You want to take this outside?'

He stopped. He laughed—a deep crackle of a laugh—kissed her deeply; buried his head in her neck.

'You got off lightly that time, Jackson.'

They stood panting, smiling.

She slid down and stood toe to toe with him, looked up at him.

He ran his hands through her hair, smoothed it down and held her jaw.

'But I'm serious. You're on *my* watch and you'll do what you're told.'

'And I'm serious too. *I* say what happens to me—nobody else.'

'We can talk about that.'

'Okay,' she said. 'I won't run off. But I don't have time to waste. I need to get a job. I don't live like this—I don't wear Gucci and slurp champagne. I've got to start looking for a job. So, unless you know of anyone hiring in Montauk, I'd rather cut my losses and head to New York. I promise I'll be back on Sunday to meet my mom.'

He stared at her.

'You need to be looked after.'

'Come on, Marco—I'm fine. I'm resilient. Look at me—I landed on the hood of your car and bounced! How resilient is *that*?'

'You still haven't got it, have you? I am responsible for you and I don't shirk my responsibilities.'

She opened her mouth. He put his finger on it.

'And, that aside, I'm enjoying your company. I'd like it if you'd stay around a bit longer. Stay around until after this deal is closed.'

He smoothed her cheek. Pressed another kiss to her lips.

She closed her eyes. 'I need a job, Marco.'

'You'll get a job. No problem.'

'I need a job and I need to start paying you back. I'm grateful for what you did, but I would have no self-respect if I let it ride. You understand that, right?'

From the kitchen came the sounds of crockery crashing on the tiled floor. Shouts rang out in Italian. Swing doors banged open and closed. Someone hurried along the passageway, his voice urging quiet and calm.

'Sure. I understand. And I'm sorry you've had it so tough.'

'I don't want your sympathy, Marco—that's the last thing I want.'

'I don't deal in sympathy. That's not my style. But I *do* know how to make money. And it just so happens I'm hiring. Come on,' he said, and he closed his fingers over hers. 'Let's eat while I tell you the Ts and Cs.'

CHAPTER SIX

THREE MILES OFF, the Montauk Point lighthouse stood proud against the pastel-hued dawn sky. Marco pounded the surf, heels catching in the incoming tide, saltwater splashing at his legs and his shorts. The cool spring wind whipped his face and chilled his lungs with each panting breath. He should be exhausted—he'd run three miles at a sprint already—but he was going to reach the Point and then turn back and do it all over again. Physical effort was the only thing that was going to keep him sane now.

Physical effort and nailing Chisholm down so tight there wouldn't be room for him to twitch so much as an eyelid. He had to sell it to him—*had* to. There was no other way. He'd offer him double what the place was worth—and double that again if he had to. And again.

It should be the simplest, sweetest deal. But nothing would surprise him in this life. That was why he had left nothing to chance. Nothing except having Stacey Jackson as third wheel, of course.

There was nothing he could do about that. He'd never shirk his responsibilities.

Yeah, and he never crossed his own boundaries.

Except last night. He'd crossed them so far he could barely see them in the distance.

But it had felt right at the time. It had felt entirely natural to subdue her like that. He knew he had been rough—he'd been wild with a need for her—and she'd loved it. He'd never known a woman like Stacey. She left the others standing. They were like a damp day before her brilliant sunshine. Hot and steamy—a tropical storm. And who knew what kind of weather would accompany that?

Who knew? *He* did! Of course he knew—she'd been that high pressure hurtling across his life once before, and she would be again if he let her. Women like Stacey were few and far between but they were high-maintenance. He'd have done anything for Stacey back then—back when he was a kid. But he'd been around the block a few times since, and he knew if he let himself slip back into that obsession just where it would end.

That said, he was going to see this through. There was always going to be a 'them'. Once upon a time he'd sworn it was going to be a long-term thing. But a one-night deal was good too. Call it his just deserts. That was what *he* was calling it now. It was the only way to get back on track. It was inevitable they were going to get it together. But it would be under *his* conditions. He would be calling the shots—the time and place.

And the time and place would be after the deal. When the whole thing was stitched up, nailed down, ticked off. That was when he'd know he was truly back on track. Beholden to nobody. And that was when he would let loose his Stacey Jackson obsession. She was the prize he'd wanted back then and it seemed pretty damn apposite that he should collect now.

Ahead, the Polo Club came into view. He slowed his pace and checked his watch—still early. Not even seven. He looked over to the stable block, where a few cars were out front. People came early to ride their horses before work. He'd get in a ride later. Maybe Stacey would like to join him.

Stacey. His mind kept drifting back there.

He'd made sure she was comfortable in her room before he'd said a curt goodnight, and before he'd slipped out this morning he'd stood at the door and listened for the steady in and out of her breathing. It was still less than twenty-four hours since the accident and she had another seventy-two under his watch. Her mother should be back in town by then anyway, and if she chose to take up the offer of a job here at the club then she'd be under his watch for even longer.

He checked his watch again, worked out his pace. That had been a good run. He should be pleased. But his gut was so tense with what was ahead that he couldn't think of anything other than getting in the shower and working out his angle if Chisholm attempted to throw him any curve balls.

He took the steps three at a time and paused on the portico as the glass doors slid open.

At the end of the day all Chisholm could do was say yes or no. And if he said no he had to be hanging out for more money, right? What other reason could there be for not selling? Marco hadn't been stupid enough to offer up more than the market value in his initial bid, but he had more than enough reserves to blast any reluctance out of his path. So, yeah—it was all going to be fine. The champagne could go on the ice—no sweat.

'Morning, hottie.'

Stacey. In Lycra. Hair in a ponytail and with a fresh-scrubbed shiny face. She looked incredible.

'Well, hi—where are you off to? Yoga?'

She smiled and waved a yoga mat under his nose.

'Wow, you're good. Solved any other mysteries this morning?'

'I happen to have solved the mystery of who could be your boss and manage you without having an aneurysm.'

Her eyes widened and her smile brightened. 'You have? You've got a job for me? You know what I said last night—I don't want your charity, Marco—it had better be a *real* job. Not just terms and conditions.'

'It *is* a real job. And if you'll give me a couple of hours I'll tell you all about it.'

She opened her mouth and closed it again. Then slid him that sly lopsided smile—the one she kept very well hidden. The one he really enjoyed seeing.

'But first I've gotta get it together. Meeting Preston at eight and *you've* got to find the yoga studio, which will be—' he pointed off down the hallway '—along there and past the pool. Keep going,' he shouted after her, 'until you've rebalanced all your chakras!'

Stacey waved her rolled up mat in the air and sauntered off. He folded his arms and watched that perfect backside, perfectly outlined in clingy leggings, her long perfect legs and that don't-give-a-damn walk. Was he mad to give her employment here?

He frowned.

He damn well hoped not. This place was too precious to him. It wasn't just any old polo club—it was a dream-come-true for him and his best friend Dante.

He walked through the lounge. Short, squat club chairs in dark blues and purples were arranged in groups around long, low coffee tables. Later they'd be full of people lounging about, eating sandwiches, drinking beer and coffee, gazing out to the ocean or the polo fields beyond. He was fond of this room—fond of the whole place. He and Dante had spent a lot of time planning it all out before they'd opened the doors a year ago. Every detail was important. Including the staff. *Especially* the staff.

Marco reached the end of the west wing and

pushed open the doors of his suite. He and Dante had one each, on either side of the main building. And soon he'd be adding the most important real estate of all to his portfolio. Yes, in less than an hour now he'd be breakfasting on coffee and eggs and a feeling of immense satisfaction as this ten-year obsession was finally put to rest.

As soon as she entered the yoga studio Stacey knew it had been a bad idea. Despite it being only seven-thirty in the morning the place was packed out, and there was only one space left at the front. She padded across the floor, rolled out her mat and sat down. A little bell rang and she looked up to smile at the teacher. And there in the mirror, eyes on stalks, were two or maybe three faces she'd hoped never to see again.

Stacey down-dogged and table-topped and made like a mountain. She did all the poses as best she could. But with every out-breath she could feel the interest along the row. It was just like school. Exactly like school.

Stopping for water, they gathered like little drones and there it was again—the background buzz that had been the soundtrack to her childhood. She heard her name. She saw them turn, a little group of two or three. Whispers, then stares, then whispers again.

What was she going to do about it? What *could* she do about it? Nothing. She wasn't going to let a bunch of gossips get her down. So she was 'that

Jackson girl'. So what? She did nobody any harm. As long as they minded their business, she would mind hers.

The class ended and Stacey rolled up her mat, sauntered back through the room, her chin up, eyes front, shaking out her hair from its clip and letting the world know with every pore of her being that they meant nothing to her. *Nothing.*

Behind her she could still hear the buzz.

'Is that really her? What is she even *doing* back here?'

'Do you think Marco knows she's here?'

'Omigod—do you think she's going to try to seduce him all over again?'

'Shut up! Marco wouldn't go *near* her now.'

Laughter.

On she went, through the club, past the swimming pool and its water aerobics class with women bobbing about to a disco beat, their coach in white shorts and white polo shirt, flirting and flattering.

On she walked as her heart rattled out its angry beat, steadying slowly with each passing step. How many times had she been in that situation before? People talking about her as if she couldn't hear them. Judging her with rules they made up as they went along.

Back out into the foyer, she saw to the left the restaurant, with its fat chairs full of fat cats having their breakfast. To the right the bar and lounges, and access to the private suite where she'd spent the night. Marco would be neck-deep in his deal with Chisholm now. He had enough on his mind. The last thing he needed was her storming in to the middle of it.

But she should talk to him. Really she should.

Every part of her wanted to cut and run. Just when she'd thought she might find something nice about Montauk after all she'd rolled over a stone and that lot crawled out from under it. There was no way she was going to get caught up in it again.

He'd understand. He'd get it.

Wouldn't he?

'Well, well, well. If I hadn't heard the news I wouldn't have believed it to be true. But here she is—Stacey Jackson. All grown up.'

Something about the tone made the hairs on her neck stand up, and she stopped in her tracks with her hand on the door.

'Aren't you going to say hello?'

She turned. *Here we go again,* she thought.

'Preston.'

He stood there—bigger, broader, hair a bit lighter, smile a bit straighter. But the eyes were as narrow and cold as ever before. Eyes that he let drift over her whole body, as if he was dragging his fingertips over her, smearing her with his own particular brand of grease.

She folded her arms defensively.

'I must say you are a sight for sore eyes, Stacey. Always were.' He whistled and smiled and drew his eyes all over her again. 'Won't you join me for a coffee?'

She hugged her arms tighter and stuck her chin higher.

'No. Thanks. I won't keep you.'

'Oh, you're not keeping me at all. I'm done.'

Stacey looked at him. Then she looked past him. Where was Marco?

'Yes, nothing keeping me here. Unless you'd like to join me?'

Stacey had opened her mouth to tell him to take a hike, the way she always had in the past, when Marco appeared around the corner.

His face was utterly, rigidly neutral, but she knew. Oh, yes, she *knew*. He was buttoning it down tight— way too tight.

'Everything okay, Stacey?' he said, his mouth a grim slash. 'Just head back to the suite and I'll catch you up about the other stuff later.'

'You never told me *Stacey* was your guest here, Marco. That puts a whole new slant on things. I may stick around a little longer. What do you say, Stacey? Care to join me for lunch? Or dinner?'

'I don't think so. I'm going to be busy sticking needles in my eyes.'

He threw his head back and laughed.

'You always had the best lines, Stacey.'

'And you always had the worst. Excuse me.'

She brushed through the middle of them. Red rage blinded her—who the *hell* did he think he was?

The same smug face, the same supercilious tone. He had no grace, no manners, no charm at all. Yet another one of the privileged who'd decided his money bought him a right to judge.

'That's a shame,' he called after her. 'We could have talked over the good old days.'

Stacey kept walking. 'That wouldn't take long.'

Yes, he and those perfect yoga bods back there— they'd all had their turn…all of them. Mocking her and making up lies about her. And Preston had always been hanging around in the background—always watching, always waiting.

'Or we could talk over the future—Marco wants to make me an offer for the Meadows. *You* could persuade me to sell it to him.'

'I've already made you an offer, Preston. A damned good one.'

Stacey heard the calm in Marco's voice and stopped. Preston Chisholm was a slimy piece of trash. Worst of all the sewer rats. But Marco wasn't. Marco had been good to her. All he wanted was to get back what was his. And all that was standing in the way was this loser.

She turned.

'Maybe I will.' She nodded to Marco, who was watching the scene with utter detachment. He frowned his answer to her.

'Keep out of my business,' he said, with a slant of his eyes.

She ignored him. 'On condition it's a table for three.'

Preston shrugged his shoulders. 'As long as Marco picks up the tab,' he said, sniggering at his own stupid joke. 'Let's eat at Betty's. Seven?'

'We'll eat here. Eight o'clock,' said Marco.

He nodded curtly to Preston and then grabbed Stacey by the elbow.

'Let's you and I have a word,' he said, leading her off.

CHAPTER SEVEN

'WHAT THE HELL do you think you're doing?' he asked, swinging her round by the hand as they entered the suite. 'This is nothing to do with you, Stacey. He's a sleazy piece of crap and no number of dinners is going to change that.'

'You told me on the way here that this was the deal of your life. Either it is or it isn't—and if it is then why would you have a problem with a dinner, for God's sake?'

'I don't have a problem with dinner—I have a problem with *you*. This is *my* deal and I don't need anyone's help.'

'You don't trust me—is that it? You think I'll say something or do something stupid.'

'No, Stacey, that's not it. It's got nothing to do with how smart you are. It's… It's…'

'Oh, get over yourself, Marco. You think because I work in casinos I can't string a sentence together?'

'Stacey, I know that you're more than capable of stringing lots of sentences together—that's the trouble. You don't take people at face value—you take them on, period. You think everything is an attack and so you go into full-blown combat mode. And with Preston Chisholm—much as I'd like to take the guy out myself—I can't risk it. I can't risk that we'll go for dinner and you'll fly off the handle because he looks at you the wrong way or—or says the wrong thing.'

As he spoke he trailed his eyes over her body. Fleetingly. Who could blame the guy for looking at her? Standing there in skin-tight leggings and a tiny little top. Her hair pulled back and her face scrubbed clean. Long, strong legs all the way down to her perfect cherry-red-painted toes. She was—simply gorgeous. But she couldn't handle it. And he couldn't risk her shooting her mouth off—or worse.

It turned out that Chisholm Junior was a worse piece of garbage than his old man. He'd turned up for coffee and stuffed his face with eggs. He'd eaten his fill and then sat back while Marco made his pitch. They both knew Chisholm Financial didn't *need* to sell. They both knew that Marco was prepared to pay way more than the house was worth.

Maybe he'd been naïve to think that he'd be able to appeal to Preston on an emotional level, if not a financial one. He'd been honest about that, at least, and all it had got him was, *'Pity your old man took such a gamble on the place.'*

Then he'd stood up, tossed his napkin on his plate and walked out. Right into the path of Stacey.

So now he knew he was going to play a game. He was going to string him along, and Marco had to learn his stupid rules if he wanted to win. And there was nothing surer on this earth than that. But adding Stacey into this was just not going to happen.

'Are you crazy? Don't you remember Betty's all those years ago? The day he sat there gawping at you for hours while you waited on tables. And I got so mad I pulled him out to the yard! And then you launched an attack on *me*. As if it was all *my* fault. What a disaster that was!'

Her eyes opened wide and then she pursed her lips and frowned, as if she was reframing her memories and seeing her so-called *I can look after myself* attitude as something negative for the first time ever. He used the silence to keep going. There was no way in hell he was letting her loose near this.

'Look, there's no other way of saying it. I saw the way he looked at you just now. He's more in love with you than ever—and that's without the two large glasses of red that he'll neck at dinner. You sit opposite him—' he gestured towards her chest '—looking like you do, and God only knows where it'll end up.'

'Ah. *That's* it.' Her face flushed with colour and fire danced in her eyes. 'It's about how I look, isn't it? Once a tramp always a tramp—is that it, Marco?'

He puffed out an angry breath. What the hell did she expect him to say to that? He wasn't going to stand in judgement on anyone, but she was hardly the most conservative type. God knew how he'd kept his cool all day while she'd stretched and rolled around inside that dress. She was who she was, and that was fine. *Fine!* But he didn't want to subject himself to another second of it until the deal was in the bag—particularly with a sleazeball like Preston Chisholm Junior anywhere nearby.

'Don't be ridiculous,' he said, trying to keep his voice low. 'Preston Chisholm would be all over you if you were dressed in a sack. We both know that.'

'Good job you didn't stick a sack in with the rest of your charity shopping, then, isn't it?'

'Back to that, Stacey? The clothes are yours. Do what you like with them. Burn them for all I care.'

She threw the yoga mat down on the floor like a petulant child. He almost expected her to stamp her foot.

'What's wrong—is your arsenal empty? No weapons left to fire?'

He knew he was going too far. But, dammit, the last thing he needed was to deal with her ego on top of second-guessing Chisholm.

In the quiet of the suite he waited, half aware that their voices might be carrying. Dante was due soon, and the staff would be circling. Marco liked a low profile, a quiet ride. He did *not* like drama and he did *not* let down his guard. He'd sworn he would never let himself go again—not since he'd been tossed off his own land, swinging punches and lashing out. It had taken five men to shift him—a fact that didn't make him proud.

'Well?' Are you going to call him to say you've changed your mind?' he demanded.

She drew in a breath so deep her chest rose up. Her skin glowed under the stretch of coral Lycra.

'Is that a yes? It's not like you to have nothing to say.'

For a moment she looked as if she was going to cry again. Her lip seemed to wobble. He stepped forward. Surely he hadn't hurt her. She was impervious to criticism—she was made of steel. Stronger! Nothing and nobody got her down. Wasn't that the case?

'Come on,' he said. 'I'm waiting. What are you going to fire at me next? Is it because I wouldn't sleep with you last night? Is that it? Must have been the first time *that's* ever happened.'

He'd never seen her lose it before. *Really* lose it. She seemed to turn white. Fury cloaked her face. She took one step and raised her arm to strike him. He caught it, brought it down by her side, pulled her in so close he could see the trail of freckles on her brow that had developed there the day before. Tiny, light and brown, sprinkled over her clear, pale skin.

'You absolute *bastard*. I wouldn't sleep with you if you were the—'

'Last man alive? Yeah, well—maybe you won't have to worry about that. I've got no intention of offering myself up for *that* particular honour.'

They stood facing each other, his hand still encircling her arm. Her breath was shallow, her mouth an angry line. Then she closed her eyes, as if looking at him was too hideous. As if they'd burn if she saw his image.

Suddenly his anger eased.

'Stacey. I'm sorry,' he said. 'I've never spoken to a woman like that before. I don't know what came over me.'

She turned away. He pulled her back round. She kept her eyes closed and tilted her head away. He loosened the grip on her arm as she twisted the rest of her body away from him.

'I mean it. I'm sorry. I didn't mean a word of that—it just came out. It must be the stress of this deal. Stacey...come on, sweetheart—you know how I feel about you...'

She stepped further away and he moved himself round to face her. He tried again to pull her close to him but she stepped away. And then she lifted her chin and her chest and seemed to suck in a breath. She straightened, and this time she faced him, and her cheeks were wet with tears.

He was appalled. He had never made a woman cry like that before. Never used words in anger. He felt sick to the pit of his stomach.

'Honey—'

'Get your hands off me, Marco.' She hissed the words at him.

'No,' he said.

He'd been fine—he could handle Chisholm and all his brinksmanship. He didn't need her help. Why

couldn't she see that? Why did she get him all fired
up like this?

He pulled her closer, so that she was right under
his face. Her eyes were glassy, the dark blue irises
glazed grey with her tears. He stared from one to the
other, saw salty smears trailing her cheeks.

'I hate you,' she said, each word a dagger.

'So you keep saying,' he said. And he pulled her
against him, grabbed her and tugged her closer than
close. 'And I'm telling you to get in line.'

'I can't see the line past the members of your fan
club,' she spat back.

He laughed. 'You are the smartest, sexiest woman
I've ever met, Jackson.'

He kept her there, fighting the urge to kiss her.
The next time he started that it was going to end in
bed. And it was too soon, yet. Much too soon.

'I mean it—get your hands *off* me!'

With another tug she loosened herself from his
grip and he let her go. Her eyes blazed with fury and
her cheeks were high with colour. She was the most
passionate woman he had ever met.

'You honestly think you can talk to me like that?
Bring me down and make me feel worse than anyone—*anyone*—has ever made me feel and that's all
right?'

He swallowed, and it was as if a boulder had
lodged in his throat. She was right.

'You know, I *nearly* ran out of here earlier. I nearly
thought *sack this*. I went to that studio and who do I

see but all your old crowd in their safe little cliques? All reassuring themselves that they've made all the right choices—the right hair and the right clothes. The right husbands and houses. Probably the right damn children. I nearly let them get to me again.'

Her eyes filled up. He moved to her. She was crying again and it was all his fault.

'Stacey—' he began, reaching out for her.

She put up her hand. He paused. Her anger and her grief grew and tears spilled freely down her face.

'No!' she said. 'I nearly let them derail me again. But I didn't. I looked at them—all of them wondering what shade of Lycra they should wear, as if that's the important stuff in life. As if their brand of trainers is more important than putting food on the table. Looking down at people like me because we have to actually *work* for a living.'

He'd heard her say things like this before. He knew how she felt about people looking down on her. But she'd never levelled her criticism at *him* before.

'You know that's not what I feel, Stacey. You know I hold you in as much regard as any of them— any—'

'Any *what*, Marco? Any woman? Because it seems to me that something's changed. You might be rich—richer than anyone in your family has ever been before—and you've got everything you could ever want. Look at you. Wealth and power ooze from every pore. But you've lost something along the way.'

'Don't be ridiculous, Stacey. I've grown up. Matured. That's all it is.'

'If that's all it is then you were better off before. Better off poor. Because the poor Marco—the one who lost it all—*he* was a nice guy. This one…'

She wiped at her eyes and turned away from him, bent down to pick up the yoga mat from the floor that had unravelled like a long pink tongue.

'I don't know what's happened to you. You always took things easy. Sure, you could get angry from time to time—but you never got personal. You never aimed to kill. But now…'

He watched as she stooped and began to roll the mat up. Watched as her back rippled with her graceful moves. Watched as her slender arms reached out and her long fingers clenched round the edges.

'What are you doing? Leave that,' he said. It was the most surreal thing. 'That's a load of crap, Stacey. You can't say that and then start rolling up your damn mat.'

'You think because you bought me a bunch of fancy clothes and made a promise to my mom that you can order me about?'

She stayed crouched down. Her fingers slipped and the mat unfurled itself.

He couldn't take it any more. He grabbed her arm and hauled her to her feet. And she let him.

'For the last damn time—the clothes are yours because I pronged you on the hood of my car. You can sue me, if you like. Others would. That's how the world is these days—so I'm grateful to you that you haven't threatened me with that...'

He knew as he finished the sentence that he hadn't finished it well. He'd let it trail. He knew and she knew—and she looked up at him.

'Yet? Did you forget to add on *yet*? Because that's what it sounded like. You actually think that I might file some sort of suit against you?'

'It wouldn't be the first time,' he said as he turned away.

'Wow,' she said. 'Now we're *really* getting somewhere.'

He walked away from her and that stupid mat. He needed coffee. There was a machine in the suite's kitchen he hardly used—he preferred going down to the restaurant kitchen and making his espresso at the huge Italian machine there. He loved the steam and the clunks of metal. The whole process of making coffee rather than just pushing a button. But he needed a blast of full-strength java now. In private. No onlookers.

'Don't turn your back on me, Borsatto.'

He stopped. What had she just said?

'Don't think for one minute that you can level all that stuff at me and then, when I raise the fact that you're a tiny bit suspicious of people, walk away.'

'I'm getting coffee,' he said, and started to move again.

'Thanks!' she called after him. 'That would be lovely. You're quite the host.'

'Pleasure's all mine,' he called back.

'Well, *your* version of pleasure is totally over-rated. I'm surprised none of your girlfriends have told you that!'

He shook his head and realised that his mouth had almost hitched into a smile. Through all the rage and frustration and confusion she and her one-liners always managed to make him smile.

He pulled out two cups and popped two coffee pods into the machine. He felt her come in to the kitchen—her presence, her aura, whatever the hell it was. But something deep within him recognised it and warmed to it. It had back then. And it did now.

He waited, hands braced on the worktop, listening to the muffled gurgles as the coffee brewed. Then he passed her the first cup and turned.

'I'm sorry,' he said again. 'Truly I am. I know it's no excuse, but Chisholm is playing games and I let that get to me. Okay?'

She took the cup and put it down.

'No. It's *not* okay. Number one—I nearly ran out of here earlier. I was all set to get on the train. And then I thought, *Actually, you know, Marco is a nice guy and he doesn't deserve to be treated badly.* You know that I only said I'd go to dinner with Preston for *you*, don't you? Number two—' She held up her hand to stop him from speaking. 'Let me finish.'

'Go on,' he said, stifling another tiny smile as he lifted the second cup from the machine and settled himself back against the worktop.

'Number two—it was *you* who lost control in Betty's, not me. I didn't give a damn that Preston was hanging out and sucking on the same soda all day. *You* had the problem with it—not me. So if anyone is going to let themselves down at dinner tonight it's you, sweetheart!'

He swallowed the espresso in two gulps, put the cup down. Gently.

'May I speak now? Or is there a number three?'

'Yeah—it just so happens there is. Number three— you have significant—and I mean *significant*—trust issues. Do not interrupt me. If you think that I would ever, *ever* come after you for damages...'

She lifted her own cup and placed it to her lips. Sipped, put it down. Gave her head a little shake and lifted her chin.

'And I can't help you with that. You need professional help to get over it.'

He couldn't hold back any more. His face broke out into a full smile and a chuckle gurgled up in his throat.

She spun round.

'What is so funny?'

He shook his head.

'Nothing. It's...'

He pushed himself back from the counter and stepped round it, braced his arms on either side of where she still leaned. She tipped her body away from him, held herself rigid.

'You. You're one of the only people I know who says it like it is.'

'It's the only way to say it.'

He nodded. 'No games with you, Stacey. Never have been and I don't suppose there ever will be.'

'None. But never mind that. Question is—how are you going to get past your paranoia that I'm going to stab Preston to death with my stiletto? Or bury you in lawsuits for dangerous driving?'

'This is my business, Stacey. My life—my deal. It's not that I don't trust you—it's just that I don't need...'

'You've got a better plan?'

He lifted his empty cup, put it back down.

'Not yet.'

'Well, what harm could it do? *Filet mignon* and a bottle of Château Lafite. Preston *likes* me. And I don't think he's all that sweet on you.'

'Any wine on the table will be Italian.'

Marco rolled it around in his head. To be truthful he hadn't yet figured out the next step in his plan. He had focused on walking out of the restaurant with the deeds to his house—hadn't let any other thought enter his head. So *now* what did he do? Smoke him out? Threaten him? Ruin him financially so there was no other choice? That wasn't his style.

'You know, the thing about Preston is that he wants to *belong*. In a way he's just like me,' Stacey said.

'How do you mean?'

'Have you ever been the one who didn't get chosen for a game? Or had literally nobody to talk to all weekend?'

Marco popped another pod in the machine as he

continued to stare at her. 'Are you truly trying to make me feel *sorry* for him?'

'No. I think he's a worthless piece of trash. But if you understand *why* he's such a creep that will help you figure out how to beat him.'

'Go on,' he said.

'He's lonely. I know how lonely feels, and he is lonely, all right. It's the most horrible way to be. He wants to be *you*. He wants to have the money and the looks and the fans and the friends. But he can't have it—so all he can do is hold back the thing you want most.'

Marco drained the second espresso in a single gulp and made yet another mental note to move to decaf.

'This is not about my ego.'

'God, no—it's about playing him at his own game. He hasn't figured out yet that being Marco Borsatto isn't all it's cracked up to be. So you let him in a little—you share your downtime...you have dinner. With me. He likes me.'

'Forget it,' he said.

'Think of it as another little bit of charity. What harm would it do? Instead of gift-wrapped leisure wear you give him gift-wrapped personal time. I bet he rolls over for you. As long as you don't sink him with a left hook if he stares at me for too long.'

Marco poured himself some water and checked his watch. Ten-thirty. Eight and a half hours to come up with a better plan. He drained the water and stared out across the bay. He had everything. Everything he could ever want. And he'd done it himself. It was a very simple rule. You could rely on one person in life and one person only. If you stuck to that then no one let you down.

And, anyway, business did not mix with pleasure. And pleasure was overrated.

'I'm sure Preston will be quite the host.'

He looked round to see Stacey sauntering across the lounge. *Pleasure was overrated*. Was it? She would bring him pleasure, all right. He was counting on it.

'If you change your mind,' she added, 'you know where we'll be.'

Then she slung him *that* look over her shoulder, hitched her lip and slowly slipped out of sight.

CHAPTER EIGHT

WIND WHIPPED AT Stacey's hair and slipped icy fingers on her bare flesh as she cycled the last part of the road down to the beach. The memory of the stinging pain of the sea breeze was still fresh. Almost as fresh as the stinging pain of being back here at all.

The road narrowed to a path, which narrowed further to a sandy track, with tufts of grass on either side and pebbles that were big enough to knock her off balance if she wasn't watching. But she knew what she was doing and steered carefully until she saw the wooden perimeter fence. It was even more lopsided and calcified than she remembered, but she settled the shiny Polo Club bike against it, tugged up her zipper and made her way down to the shore.

The waves roared her a welcome, but it was the shingly swish of the tide back and forth, back and forth, that most brought her home. She picked her way to her favourite spot and there it was—the same flat-topped rock that she'd sat on for so many hours, just staring out across the bay at the sprawling mansions and estates opposite.

She stepped out of her trainers, buried her toes in the sand and looked directly over at the biggest estate of all—the Meadows. Even from this distance she could make out the fence that had been erected along its boundaries since she'd been away. Different parts of it had been parcelled up and sold off for retirement homes, summer houses and—according to Marco, who had almost spat out the words at dinner last night—*'Goddamn crazy golf'*.

It must really hurt, she thought. To know that what had once been your family home was now occupied by hundreds of strangers.

She'd never felt any sense of loss for the two-bed shack that *she'd* called home, though. It hadn't felt like a home since her dad had gone. That was when it had all started to go wrong. She could see it so clearly now. Her mother's whole world had been about pleasing her husband. Every decision she'd made had been run through a mental *Will he like it?* filter.

He hadn't been a bad man so much as a disgustingly selfish one. He probably hadn't set out to leave them devastated and torn apart—he'd just seen something he'd liked better and thought he'd have that instead. It wouldn't surprise her to learn that he'd moved on to wife number three by now.

Stacey scooped up a handful of sand and let it trickle through her fingers. A few gritty lumps caught in her palm and she shook them, watching the glints of quartz catch the sun. She'd watched her mother too. Waiting. Just waiting. Her whole life on pause while she waited for him to come home. Losing her beauty, her figure, her health. Wasting her life, waiting for a loser.

Because that was what he was. She'd found that out the hard way. In a way she had Marco to thank for that. Because if he hadn't asked her about the rumours she might never have run off to find him. It had been the bullet she'd needed to fire her out of town. Her wonderful father had got the hell out and she was going to do exactly the same.

If only finding him had been the crock of gold she had imagined. All she'd got instead was twenty dollars stuffed in her hand when he'd finally shown up in a little diner, because it was 'easier that way'. The slack jaw and the paunch she hadn't remembered—the restless blue eyes she had. Because they were *her* eyes—the same eyes that stared back at her every single day, reminding her of his weakness and hers.

Oh, yes, she *was* weak. Weak and selfish—just like him. And it terrified her. She would never forget the looks of disgust and disappointment on everyone's faces when she'd reappeared. The panic she'd caused. And worst of all the hurt she'd caused her mother. She had screamed at her that *she* had caused this. *She* had driven her daddy away into the arms of another woman. *It was all her fault.*

Her mother had simply bowed her head and agreed.

She would never, *ever* forgive herself for that.

She looked across the lake to the private jetty with little boats like bunting all along it, to the dense, dark wall of shrubs. Behind it, she knew now the swimming pool was dried up, tennis courts tufted with dead brown grass. A sprawling English manor house and outbuildings—stables, yards and meadows. All desperately, dreadfully vacant. And, hidden away beside the lake in the willow trees, the summerhouse—the last habitable building.

She'd had no idea what she was going to say when she'd cycled along the driveway that day, but she'd had to try. They'd been close. He'd been her friend, her confidant. Her anchor. And when their friendship had grown over those few short weeks into something deeper it had been beautiful. She'd had something beautiful in her life for the first time since her daddy had gone.

She'd wanted to make one last attempt to explain why she'd lied about the gossip. If only she'd known why herself. To hurt him? To hurt herself? Why she'd then fled to find her father. Why she'd come back. Why she'd balled up the anger at herself and fired it right back at her mother. She'd needed Marco's comfort, craved his touch, his tender words, the patience he had shown her every other time.

She'd never got the chance to reason with him, though. Two trucks had passed her as she'd cycled.

Men had jumped out, and when she'd caught up with them Marco had been yelling and swinging punches. She'd thrown down her bike and raced over, but they'd just grabbed him up and thrown him in a truck. Driven right past her.

Straight past her and straight through any hope she'd had of making things right between them…

The wind was rising. The bunting fluttered helplessly. Stacey dropped the rest of the sand and clapped her hands clean.

Yes he'd had it tough back then but things had worked out. And he deserved even more. She'd help him. Of course she would. She wanted to get one over on the Prestons of the world as much as he did—Preston Chisholm and the rest. She wanted to walk into the Polo Club lounge tonight with Marco and she wanted to feel as if she belonged there. Just for once. Just for tonight.

She flicked the last grains of sand from her palm and stood up. Then she stepped onto the rock and looked out across the wild and beautiful bay to the Meadows beyond. He *would* get it back. He'd make it his home and maybe even settle down here in time. That was his dream.

She'd had a similar dream once. She'd imagined he might fall in love with her. But that kind of thing was never going to happen, and she would be beyond insane even to let the kernel of hope seed itself in her heart.

No. She'd keep her distance—physically and emotionally. But she'd be there at his side, pulling Preston into her net. All in a good cause.

She tucked her feet back into her trainers. She was going to head back to the Polo Club now and begin to prepare for the evening ahead. She had the most exquisite dress to wear and she was going to enjoy every last second. Before the clock chimed midnight and she had to scurry back to her cinders again.

'Okay, you can have dinner with Preston tonight. But I'll be there and you'll take your cues from me. I do *not* want you talking about my house at all. Is that understood?'

Stacey clipped her earrings into place. Beautiful black pearls that played hide and seek with the light. She twisted her neck until a slick of rainbow colours wrapped itself around the little globes. Then twisted the other way and watched it darken into midnight.

'Sorry—what did you say?' She lifted the necklace next. 'Only I thought for a second you were trying to give me *permission* for something.'

'Here...let me get that.'

Marco strode across the room. She kept her gaze fixed on her earrings. Anything except look at the image of him. All that storm of a man. Snug dark jeans and tight black cashmere. Energy resonating from his core.

He lifted the necklace from her hands and slid it round her throat.

'Where were you all day? I was looking for you.'

'I'm in the clear, Marco. No headaches, no fainting. You don't need to worry about a thing.'

'I was looking for you because I wanted to see if you wanted to go riding.'

His fingers brushed her skin. Every nerve sprang to life.

'And I wanted to apologise.'

He placed his hands on her shoulders and turned her round. She let her eyes land on his mouth. Earnest and electrifying. How the hell did he do it?

She looked away.

'You look stunning. Every inch the lady.'

'Thanks,' she said aloud.

Her prayer of thanks was silent, but she'd hoped that the midnight-blue silk shift would pick out her eyes and complement her skin tone. And that the round neck was modest enough to keep everyone's gaze exactly where it should be. Her hair was pinned back at one side to give her an elegance that she desperately needed. Her skin was lightly bronzed and her eyes subtly shaded. She looked exactly the way she'd wanted to look.

His fingers found her chin, tipped it up gently.

'You've been avoiding me.'

'Hey,' she said, turning herself back around and picking up a bracelet. 'Hate to break it to you, but there *are* other attractions in Montauk.'

She tried to flick the catch open with her thumb, but it flicked back and forth aimlessly.

'What's going on, Stacey?'

She slapped the bracelet back down on the dressing table.

'You show up here, fifteen minutes before I'm due to eat dinner, and you find me clipping on earrings. What are all the clues pointing to, Sherlock?'

She wasn't going to pretend that this past hour had been easy. He'd been nowhere in sight and she'd actually begun to think that he wasn't going to show up at all. She'd been toying with ideas of how she was going to play it with Preston if he didn't show. But she wasn't going to lose it. She wouldn't do that. Cool was her MO. There was no other way.

'I've been taking care of some other bits of business. Dante's in town. He's going to join us.'

He lifted her wrist with one hand, lifted the bracelet with the other and fastened it in one smooth move.

'Ah,' she said. 'Did you give *him* permission to come to dinner too?'

'What's that supposed to mean?'

She smiled, sweet as she could.

'Nothing. It'll be nice to meet him. And I'm sure Preston will be thrilled.'

She went to move away but he held her wrist, tugged her back.

Her eyes flashed into his. He was stormy. Dark. Dreadfully sombre.

'You know, I'm still not mad about this idea at all.'

'It can be dinner for two. Just say the word.'

She was trying to be light. She tried to smile. But

the thunderous look from his eyes told her this was a man on the edge.

'Marco. You need to chill. This is PC Junior's little party—his fantasy come true. So just let me play the hostess in the way I know how, and if he drops any happy crumbs you be ready to pick them up.'

She dusted invisible dust from his chest, smoothed the muscles with her palm. Then she smoothed with her other palm. A really stupid thing to do. He felt like heaven. Her own particular version of heaven. Warm and strong and solid and safe. She breathed him in—couldn't not.

She tried to pull her hands away but he took hold of her wrists, moved a little closer.

'Stacey. Look at me.'

She fluttered her eyes up to his. It wasn't a great idea. He was like an electrical storm, and she was trying her damnedest to keep indoors with the shutters battened down.

'What?' she said, looking at his mouth. The blue-black glaze of shadow that framed it kick-started the merry little dance her body so enjoyed.

'You'll do what you're told and let *me* lead this tonight. I can't risk anything going wrong.'

He lifted a finger to the underside of her chin and gently tipped it up. His eyes fell to her mouth. He leaned forward. She desperately wanted to kiss him.

'And you have to trust me.'

His hand dropped…his head fell. He stepped

away. The eye of the storm moved off, leaving only an anxious pause before the damage could be seen.

'You don't understand.'

'I understand more than you think,' she said, grabbing his sleeve. 'I know what it's like to have something held just out of reach. To be teased over and over and think that you just *might* get it if only you do this or that or the next thing.'

He looked at her hand on his sleeve.

'Of course you do—it was how you rolled, Stacey, yeah?'

Her fingers slid from the velvety softness of the cashmere straight onto her chest to hold in a gasp of air. He was talking about *them*. He was stabbing her with the rumours even now.

'Look, I'm sorry—I didn't mean that—'

'Oh, you meant it, all right.'

All this time had passed yet he still believed the lies.

'You took it the wrong way—'

She held her hand up. 'I took it the way you said it.'

'Stop this *now*, Stacey.'

He grabbed her wrists and hauled her against him.

'You haven't a clue about me, Marco. And every time I've tried to talk to you about back then you shut me down.'

'I told you—it's not my business how you ran your life or how you run your life now. But it damned well *is* my business how I run mine.'

She kept her head twisted.

'Look, I'm sorry. I trust you, Stacey. More than I've ever trusted anyone. I don't know why, but I do.'

His voice was low. It was calm. It was the way it had used to sound. He held her close, pulled her in against him. And as they stood there, holding one another, Stacey felt the warmth and security of being in his arms, her head on his chest, listening to the steady strong sound of his heart, and inside her something tight and painful loosened.

She drew in her breath, pushed herself back, put her hands on his chest.

'Well played, there. You were almost out of aces, but you pulled it back from the brink.'

He put his hands on hers. Flattened them against his chest. Held them there.

'Not everything's a joke, Stacey. I meant what I said.'

She swallowed. 'I meant what I said too, Marco. Every word.'

'Good, then let's do this. Let's go get Sant'Angelo's back from that grifter.'

CHAPTER NINE

BEAUTIFUL WOMEN WERE a dollar a dozen in the Hamptons. They were even more common in New York. In Asia and Europe they were everywhere, too. Marco liked to find beauty in his world, and beauties made a habit of finding their way into his. He was lucky. He knew it and he'd never taken anything for granted.

When things had started to go wrong in his early teens—when the cracks had started to appear in his parents themselves, and then in their marriage, when the paintings and then the jewellery and then the house and the land itself had all had to go—even then he'd still known he was lucky.

People liked him. Men and women sought out his company. And he'd learned that when he wanted something all he had to do was really want it, really go after it, and it would land in his lap. One way or another. Sometimes women landed in his lap a lot more often than he wanted, of course.

But not this one.

As he watched her walk through the hallway to

the reception area he still couldn't believe that she was the one that got away. Sure, he was the one who had pushed her—he'd been out of his mind with jealousy when she'd admitted that the stories that had been circulating were true. He'd been so *sure* she was loyal to him. So sure that she was beginning to fall in love with him. So sure that they might actually be able to go the distance in some way or another.

He had trusted her implicitly back then—the same way that she'd seemed to trust *him* implicitly too. She'd opened up to him. She'd poured forth her heart and her head. He was the one who had counselled her through the worry about her mother.

He knew that. He'd lived it himself.

'Hey, buddy, good to see you.'

He felt Dante's hand on his back and heard the familiar mellow tones of his friend in his ear.

'Hey.' He stopped, turned and gave him the handshake, backslap and smile exchange that had marked their friendship for the past fifteen years.

'Stacey, hold up!' he called, and smiled as she turned her head in her best Lauren Bacall to slant a glance over her shoulder before turning slowly. 'Come and say hello to Dante. My partner in crime—and other things.'

She trained that navy blue gaze directly on him, and then her face broke into a full, unguarded smile—the exotic lily, so fragile, so rare. A momentary tension crept down his spine. Would Dante make more of it than he should?

But he should have known better. His friend had his back, and he knew enough about the situation to manage it perfectly. He walked forward and shook her hand. Kept his distance. Cool. Appropriate.

'A pleasure to meet you, Stacey.'

She continued to smile and—*dammit*—the smile was in her eyes too. Dante did that to people. They loved him. He was like a long drink in the desert, a blast of sunshine in the darkness. He had a light, easy manner that everyone warmed to. Marco had never minded it before.

'Let's get this started. *And* finished,' he said, moving them both through. 'Ol' Preston will be waiting.'

And sure enough there he was.

'Stacey.'

He stood, filled the space with his hulking frame and flat-topped head. Marco resisted the urge to reach over and twist his neck.

'My, but you look more and more beautiful each time I see you. Come over here and sit next to me.'

'Thanks, Preston, but I don't want to get too close,' she said smoothly, resting her hands on the back of the chair opposite. 'Nobody wants to see a grown man dribbling. The sight of saliva on a dress shirt? *Eugh*.'

Marco heard a muffled chuckle to his left from Dante, but it was drowned in the guffaw that Preston delivered as, regardless, he shifted himself forward and tried to steer Stacey round to the seat beside him.

'What a mouth you have. I'll say that. Beautiful and smart. The whole package.'

'Preston. Good to see you again.'

Dante reached across to shake his hand and everyone slipped into the heavily upholstered chairs dotted around the table. They were right in the middle of the rear wall. The place was packed—and as far as Marco could make out every head was turned.

Stacey sat back in her seat, crossed her legs and then tugged down the hem that had ridden up. So her legs weren't bare, as he'd thought, but clad in sheer silk stockings. He let his gaze travel from the lacy-topped flash of thigh down the curve of her shin to her shoes—satin, pointed and skyscraper-high.

There was *no way* Preston Chisholm was going to get his hands on those. Stacey would use them as weapons first, he thought. Still, it wasn't his business what she did with her damn shoes—but even so his hands bunched and he realised his jaw was even more tense than it had been earlier. He looked for a glass of water and realised Dante was in the throes of ordering drinks and keeping the small talk going.

'So, what have you done with yourself in the past ten years, Stacey? Last I heard you'd left the cruise ships and were in Atlantic City,' said Preston.

'Was that front page on the *Long Island News*?'

'People here like to hear how everyone's getting on. And I've always made it my business to keep up with your news. I must admit I nearly made it all the way down there once, on a whim.'

'All the way to Atlantic City? On a *whim*? A whim to do what—lose all your money?' said Stacey.

'I consider myself a very lucky guy. And if I'd run into *you* I'd have hit the jackpot.'

'And I feel so blessed that you didn't.'

Stacey crossed her legs. Marco's eyes dropped.

Preston laughed again. 'Well, I for one feel very blessed that you're back in Montauk. And for good, I hope?'

Marco spoke. 'We're not here to discuss Stacey's personal business, Preston. I'm sure we'd all be more comfortable if we kept to the agenda.'

Stacey slanted him a look, but said nothing. Preston raised his eyebrows. Marco felt his veins bubble with boiling blood. Who the *hell* did he think he was?

'Hey, man,' Dante said, leaning over. 'You want to dial down the alpha? He's no threat.'

Marco tried to puzzle out what his friend was talking about, but then his eyes slid to Stacey again. She still sat back in her chair, looking as if she was watching some dull repeat on television. One hand was on her lap, the other idly reached out for her glass of water. She took a sip, replaced it, appeared to listen to whatever Preston was droning on about and then lifted her menu, as if she had surpassed her boredom threshold entirely.

She acted like that around mostly everyone he recalled. And it infuriated the hell out of them. With him she was unguarded, open and a whole lot of woman. He doubted Preston could handle even a tenth of the *real* Stacey Jackson.

As Preston droned on Marco watched her, fascinated by the exquisite lines of her face that made up her profile. By the thick sweep of hair that she'd tucked behind one ear with a flower and the perfect ear, jaw and neck he could never tire of looking at.

'Yes, the place has changed. Definitely,' he heard her say.

He looked up. Preston was leaning forward on his elbows, gazing intently. What the hell was he looking at? Marco swivelled round to see Stacey twirling a strand of her hair as she leaned forward to lift her wine goblet. Could he see a shadow of cleavage from that angle? Marco looked back to Preston, but he was now addressing the waitress.

'You planning on sitting with your mouth like that all night?' Dante chuckled quietly as he put his own glass down on the table.

'What are you talking about?'

'I thought this was a *business* dinner. I'm sure that was what you said. Only I'm wondering when your business acumen is going to ship in. Looks like it's stuck in your pants somewhere.'

'Changed in what way, Stacey?'

Marco dismissed Dante with a frown and retuned his attention to the other conversation.

'Well, the Meadows, of course. That hideous fence that's wrapped right around the front of it. I saw it from across the lake this morning.'

Preston laughed.

'I don't know what you find so funny, Preston. The one thing this town's got going for it is its history. And that real estate's a prime example—if we don't preserve that, what happens? Regardless of who owns it, there should be greater care taken over what it's used for. It's right next to a national park. What's next? Knock down the lighthouse and put up a high-rise?'

She took a sip of wine and turning her attention to the waitress circling the table, placed her order. And all the while Preston watched her. And all the while Marco watched him.

'Well, now, Stacey, I'm sorry you think that. What do you think the people of Montauk *should* be doing to make a living, then?'

'I don't see any problem in them doing what they used to do. Keeping the integrity of the place. Atlantic City it ain't—and nor should it be.'

'You have to agree that Stacey has a point,' said Dante.

Marco looked around.

'But Preston is right too—the place has to keep pace with what people want. That way folks can make a living without upsetting what made the place great to start with.'

'I'd hardly call what you're doing "making a living", Preston,' said Stacey.

'But that's exactly what I *am* doing, missy.'

'*Missy*?' drawled Stacey, raising her eyebrows. 'Did we slip back into the nineteenth century when I wasn't looking?'

The awkward moment was punctuated by two

large platters of oysters appearing in the centre of the table and a bustle of plates and glasses. There was a dozen on each, opened and lying on crystals of ice, flanked by lemon and smelling like a sea breeze.

'Well, I'm sorry, I'm sure—I really didn't mean to offend you, Stacey—'

'You didn't,' cut in Marco. 'Offend her. That's Stacey's idea of a joke.'

Marco bit down on his frustration. He could feel the whole deal sliding into a black hole. He knew it. He'd known this whole idea was a disaster. He had to cut it short. He turned to Stacey to make a 'cut' sign. But she was staring at him as if she wanted to kill him. Didn't she see what was happening? What the hell was she playing at?

'Oh, I don't mind at all. Won't you have an oyster, Stacey?' asked Preston, lifting the platter in her direction.

'She doesn't like them,' Marco heard himself say.

Stacey twisted round in her seat and drew his eyes to hers. 'No, but she *does* answer for herself.'

'That's exactly what I'm afraid of.'

Without a pause she lifted her napkin and tossed it onto the table. Then she stood. Preston stood too, followed by Dante and then Marco.

'Why don't I go and powder my—*mood* while you tuck in to your seafood? And do go on—sit yourselves down. The feminists didn't burn their bras for nothing, you know.'

And then she took herself and her attitude and swayed and swished her way off to the ladies' room.

Dante was the first to sit.

'It's great to meet a woman with character. She'd get along great with Lucie—that's for sure,' he said.

'She's amazing,' said Preston.

Marco tried and failed to unbunch his fists.

'The oysters are terrific,' said Dante.

'I'll be right back,' said Marco.

He tossed his own napkin down and followed the trail of eyes through the tables and out into the foyer.

At the ladies' room he stopped and waited. He put his hand on the door and then pulled it back. He paced up and down. An elderly couple came towards him—friends of his parents. He tried to smile, then stood back to let them past. They stopped, wanted to chat.

The door opened.

'Excuse me,' he said curtly, and he reached for Stacey. He grabbed her hand.

'What do you think you're doing?' she demanded as he tugged her along the corridor behind him. She dug her heels in and wouldn't move any further, so he stopped, spun around. Pinned her there.

'Having two minutes of your time.' He braced his hands on the wall, either side of her.

'You can have two seconds.'

'You told me you could handle this—that I could trust you.'

'Yeah?' She frowned. 'And…?'

'And,' he repeated, unable to keep the frustration out of his voice, 'you're totally out of control in there. You're playing this all wrong, and I'm going to end up with a cluster dump of a deal on my hands with no way back.'

'*I'm* playing this all wrong?' She stepped forward, into his space, put her hands on her hips. 'What are you talking about? He can't get enough of me—he *loves* how I handle him.'

'You're not handling him—you're insulting him!'

'You're insulting *me*. You really think I don't get the concept? You've only been going on and on about it for the past, like, forty-eight hours. Do you really think I'm so dumb that I would blow this deal on purpose?'

'Not on purpose, but you're going to—the way you're talking. And acting.'

'Acting like what?'

'Acting like the Big I Am. His teenage crush come to life.'

'Oh, get over yourself. Why don't you sit back and relax for once? Have a little faith in somebody other than the Amazing Marco Borsatto.'

A crowd of women came down the corridor, tripping along on high heels and giggles, their eyes on stalks at the sight of them sharing what must look like an intimate moment.

She shook her head and went to push past him.

She was going back in there to wrap Preston up in

her feminine wiles. It could go one way or the other. And he couldn't risk the other.

'Excuse me,' she hissed.

He didn't budge. He felt her body brush against him, hot and soft. The same body that Preston Chisholm was going to drool over while she mangled this deal until it was dead in the water.

He put his hand on her waist and spun her against his side, facing the opposite direction.

'Let's do this in private.'

'What the…?'

His office was straight ahead—he began to stride.

'You and I need some time alone.'

'I'm on a date,' she said, pushing herself away from him.

He gripped her tightly. 'You're *my* date. And you're out of line. This ends now.'

'Get off!' she said, but he gripped her tighter still, until her heels left the ground and he was carrying her, clamped to his side.

On they went, past the pool, its ghostly blue water eerily still, luminous, deserted. A gym class was finishing in one of the studios. People spilled out, guzzling water from bottles, smiling and laughing. He rounded the corner to where a mobile display unit splashed pictures of Montauk's outdoor pursuits—riding, swimming, fishing, pink-cheeked faces beaming with the joy of all that fresh air. *His* face was set in a tight, tense mask.

Stacey spat her fury in angry whispers. He yanked her tighter and strode on.

On down the hallway, past the physio rooms and the therapists' suites. Everyone was gone. Everything was silent—except for his breath and her curses, and the sound of blood rushing in his ears, and the feel of her clasped hard against his body.

'In here.'

He stopped at the door that led to his office, flung it open and spun them both inside.

'You've gone too far this time Stacey. Far too far.'

She stood facing him, hands at her sides, staring at him, her chest heaving with deep breaths.

'*I'll* decide where I go and how far and who with and everything else—not you! And you *won't* judge me or answer for me—got it?'

Her eyes sparkled in the gloom of the room. Her face glowed and her teeth gleamed.

'Your problem is nobody ever disciplined you. Nobody ever took you in hand and showed you who was boss.'

Her hands went to her hips and she threw back her head. 'You think you're the one? You think you're going to "discipline" me now? Is that it?'

Suddenly he could think of nothing other than that.

He took a pace towards her.

'That *is* it. I'm going to take you in hand and teach you some respect. Teach you some manners.'

She laughed, but there was no mirth in it. There was challenge. There was promise.

'You wouldn't dare.'

'You crossed the line. I trusted you to behave and you crossed the line.'

'So what are you going to do about it? Put me over your knee? Spank me?'

She stared at him and every single nerve in his body vaulted to life. Blood roared in his ears. His cock throbbed and grew rock-hard.

'I'm going to do what I should have done a long, long time ago.'

His voice wasn't his own. He'd lost the last shard of control. He was in thrall to the passion that was raging through his body. He grabbed her by the hand and pulled her hard against his body.

'You like to be subdued, don't you? Hmm? Last night at the vineyard you couldn't get enough. You wanted more then, didn't you? And that's why you're flirting so hard tonight. That's why you're wearing the lingerie. You want it so badly, Stacey. It's all you ever wanted.'

She gasped and he put his mouth on hers.

He felt the softness of her lips and the fight in her spirit and it urged him on harder. He tasted her energy, her wit, her beauty, her passion. He held her steady as she tried to shift about and he laved every last inch of her mouth. His tongue rolled around inside her mouth, plundered every moist corner.

'Marco!' she cried, but he buried it with his tongue until she groaned her pleasure.

His hands grabbed her shoulders, ran down her arms to her ribs and then sealed around her breasts. He moulded and massaged and ground her nipples with his thumbs. She was screaming into his mouth but he would not give her an inch of relief.

'I think you're beginning to understand,' he said as he stepped back and looked around. He was having her here. *Now.*

With a swipe of his arm he cleared his desk of the few artefacts that sat there. They crashed to the floor. He leaned back on it.

He hauled her close, then immediately thrust her back to stand in front of him. Her hair was dishevelled, her dress awry. He put one hand on her waist, holding her exactly where he wanted her.

'Lift the dress. Right up.'

'You can't order me around—'

'Now!' he barked.

And in the fraction of a second that stretched before them he saw the years, the emotions, the kindness, the loss and the pain. He saw his beautiful friend, his teenage sweetheart. But most of all he saw the trust. Her eyes were glazed with lust and excitement. Her mouth was open and wanting. He knew and she knew that she would never, ever fall into line for anyone else.

But she did for him.

She stood with her legs open, put her hands on the skirt of her dress and began to tug it up. His eyes dropped. She inched it up. Stopped. His eyes flashed back to hers. She was challenging him.

'I didn't tell you to stop, Stacey.'

Her chest heaved and he watched her draw in a deep breath. Her tongue snaked out between her lips. Slowly she began to raise the dress again.

'You're going to be in even more trouble if you disobey me, Stacey.'

She bit her lip, looked up at him through the lop-sided swish of her hair, where the flower had loosened.

'I'm. So. So. *Sorry*,' she said.

'You don't look it,' he said back.

He'd never felt lust like this in his life. He sat on the edge of his desk—the pressure of his cock was immense.

She edged the dress up again, right to the thick edge of her stockings. Bare flesh on either side… He stifled a groan. She kept going until a shadow began to appear between her legs, and then the soft swell of the panties that covered her most private place.

'Right up. Past your panties.'

The twin tracks of a suspender belt snaked under the edges of her panties. Everything was cream, satin, drawing his eyes and his hands.

'That's more like it. Now, hold your dress up and turn around.'

For a moment her eyes telegraphed a challenge. And he answered her back—she could trust him. She *had* to trust him. There was only them.

So she closed her lids and turned for him, showing him the perfect backside that he had dreamed of and loved for all these years.

'Now, come over here. Right now.' His voice was hoarse.

She moved—away from him. Quick as a flash he grabbed her hand and tugged her back. Her laughter swirled through the air.

'Over my knee, Stacey.'

And he laid her across his knee.

Her skirt had dropped and he heaved it back up. His blood flowed like fire through his body. She wanted this—and he wanted it even more. He tugged her panties down in one smooth move. They stuck over her butt cheeks but with another tug he got them down to her thighs—and then brought his hand down on her bare flesh.

'*Now* you know who's the boss around here, hmm?'

'Yes,' she gasped. 'Yes...'

He held her dress up and stared down at the most erotic sight he had ever seen. And then he brought his hand down harder.

'Yes,' she cried. 'Again!'

'*You* don't decide what happens here, Stacey. *I* do.'

But he left his hand on her, and then he slid his fingers forward and through the soft, soaked flesh between her legs. She was velvet to his touch and he found her bud in seconds. She grasped at the desk, his legs, the air as he kept up the pressure, hard and fast, rubbing her back and forth.

She screamed his name as seconds later he brought her to orgasm.

There under his hand she quivered and groaned, and sobbed and sighed his name.

He heaved her up to her feet and unfastened his zipper. He shoved his trousers to the floor, kicked off his shoes and stepped clear. Her greedy little hands heaved at his cock, stroking it and tugging at it.

'Get rid of these,' he said, yanking at her panties.

And she did—she thrust them off and then hooked her legs around him.

'God, you drive me out of control. I *am* out of control.'

He had to find a wall, or a floor—the desk. He turned and laid her down. She slid back and yelped, and he grabbed her hips and pulled her so that he could bury himself to the hilt. He positioned himself and thrust up inside her.

He pushed into this woman. *Stacey.* He held her body in his hands and buried himself as deep and slow as he could. And then he moved faster and faster. He felt his orgasm build and then break, and he thrust his fill over and over and over, until he had nothing left to give her.

Seconds filled the space—moments of time be-fore they'd have to come to terms with what had just happened. His head began to clear and his heart slowed. He looked down. He had never seen anything so lovely. She lay before him on the desk, her hair spread out in a halo, the flower—gone. Her dress was bunched up at her ribs and she was clad only in her stockings. Wild-eyed, wide-mouthed, she lay there as she had in all his dreams.

He slid his hands under her shoulders and lifted her up.

She put her hands round his neck and hung on.

'Do you think they've missed us?' she whispered. 'How long have we been away?'

He shook his head.

'I don't know,' he said, his mind tumbling back to the dinner table—Preston and Dante, staring at one another over two platters of chilled oysters. Himself losing his head—storming out after Stacey. Preston checking his watch. Dante schmoozing with small talk—smoothing over the awkwardness of this, the so-called deal of his life.

And this—what they had just done.

He crushed his eyes closed for a moment. He had absolutely lost his mind.

He reached up his hand and smoothed her hair. He fixed her dress as best he could as she slid down his body. She picked up her panties and stepped into them. He put his clothes back on. Silently.

He wasn't stupid. That hadn't been just some quickie in the closet. That had been deep. There was something going on here that he didn't even want to think about. He'd done some interesting stuff before. Some girls liked to play—most girls didn't. But those navy eyes, when she'd looked up at him—they'd been seeking something out—he didn't even want to know what. He *really* didn't.

He was a fool. A damn fool.

'I think we'd better get back and see.'

CHAPTER TEN

A Noël Coward song was playing in the lounge as they made their way back. Light laughter bubbled up from a seating nook across the hallway. A waiter shook a cocktail maker in a fast, regular tattoo and with a one-armed flourish began to pour liquor into two wide-rimmed glasses. Behind his head a smoky mirror reflected their progress—Marco's sure, proud stride and Stacey's cat-like prowl.

A five-minute stop-off in the suite and she was presentable again. At least on the outside. The cacophony of emotions and hormones within was something else entirely. Words might have helped, but the dense, silent fog that had slipped over them had almost blinded her.

It was all she'd been able to do to put one foot in front of the other, to follow through on defaults like fixing the red lipstick that had been smeared pink all around her mouth, brushing the hair that had been in a haze of tugs and frizz, and simply trying to move around in the world the way she had for the past twenty-six years when it felt as if she had tumbled into someone else's.

As they neared their table she could see Dante in profile. He saw them enter a second before Preston did.

Preston stood. 'Call off the search party! She's back!' he called out.

Nobody laughed.

'We didn't wait—figured you'd had second thoughts about the oysters,' said Dante, casting a curious glance over them both.

Stacey turned her face to the side and swallowed as she slid into her seat. Marco stayed standing, chest out, and looked around the room as if checking it was still there. Then he looked down at Stacey, pulled out his chair and sat. Slowly.

'The oysters weren't the greatest idea you've ever had,' he said.

'Is everything all right, Stacey?' Preston was looking at her with unguarded concern.

'She's fine—' began Marco.

Stacey looked up sharply.

'Yes—you answer for yourself. I know.'

She looked straight at Preston. 'I'm fine.' She looked at Marco. 'Thanks.'

Stacey reached for her glass. Her fingers had stopped shaking, but her heart was still thundering and she doubted it would ever stop. How on earth would life settle back to normal after what she'd just done? Not only had she stepped over the line with Marco, she'd stepped over the line with herself.

She read magazines—she knew sex could be crazy. But she'd never wanted any part of that kind of scene. She'd never really wanted part of *any* kind of scene. It was what it was. She knew that some women faked orgasms. She never had. Maybe she'd faked desire…

But not tonight.

This—this was beyond exciting. This was desire such as she'd never felt before. She had never, *ever* felt so hot and so tuned in to another person. She'd never given herself, followed instructions, become submissive. It had felt completely exhilarating. She'd felt alive.

'Stacey, I'm determined we won't chase you away again. What do I need to do to keep you here?'

'Talk about real estate,' she said smoothly, rubbing her finger over a red mark on her wrist. 'It's on point, I hear.'

Preston chuckled and sat forward, beamed her a smile and then beckoned to the waiter.

Stacey crossed her legs, the bare skin of her thighs rubbing in a reminder of what she'd just done. Now—sitting in company—she felt an echo of that thrill. She shifted her legs again, enjoying the sensation of satin on skin, and relived that moment of lifting her dress up. That look in his eyes—hungry, desperately wild and totally in command. Just thinking of that moment sent another pulse to her core and she shifted again.

Marco was right beside her. Her eyes landed on his thighs—muscled and strong and long. He might be sitting knees apart, in that relaxed way he always did, but he was tense. He was edgy. He was giving off such a commanding vibe that she found it hard to focus.

'Let's have champagne. The finest you have.'

Stacey snapped back to the moment.

'What are we celebrating?' she asked, fixing Preston with a slight smile. 'Did you just agree to sell the Meadows while I was powdering my nose? Way to go, PC.'

She felt Marco bristle beside her. She saw Dante turn. She heard Preston chuckle again as he lifted a bread roll and started to butter it.

'All in good time,' he said. 'The champagne is because I'm celebrating seeing *you* again after all these years. Real estate is stones and dirt. You're flesh and blood. Luscious and lovely. So much more interesting to talk about.'

'Okay. That's it. I'm through.' Marco tossed his napkin down on the table.

Stacey felt her head swivel on her neck as she turned to stare at him properly for the first time since they'd left his office. He was like a force of nature. He looked like some fierce, dark elemental being. He looked for all the world as if he was going to rip Preston limb from limb. His high cheekbones were stained, his mouth was parted and his shoulders held pure, hard tension.

He stood.

'Hey, buddy! Good idea—let's get some air. I need to talk to you.'

Dante stood too. He put his arm out to clasp Marco's, but he'd already pushed himself back from the table.

'Enjoy yourselves,' he said. 'But not on my account.'

And he turned and walked away.

Dante made to go after him and then looked back.

'Stay right where you are,' he said, turning to stare at Stacey, the lightness in his voice belied by the intent in his eyes. 'We've got a couple of things to go over and then we'll be right back.'

Preston sat back in his chair and beamed. He steepled his fingers and stared at Stacey. Stared in that way he had that unsettled her stomach.

'Well, now. Looks as if we're left to our own devices, Stacey. Looks like someone couldn't quite handle the way things were headed.'

'What are you trying to say, Preston?'

'Oh, come on now, Stacey. You're not a stupid girl. You can see clearly what kind of person Marco Borsatto really is, can't you? He may have made a lot of money, but he can't cover up those genes. The man's one step away from total meltdown. Just like his father—and *his* father before him.'

Stacey lowered the glass of water she'd been sip-

ping from. She had to be careful or she might launch
it at him.

'I'm sorry, Preston. I'm not following you.'

He sat forward. Reached across the table for
the hand she'd used to cradle the glass. His fingers
closed round hers.

'I don't think so,' she said, nailing him with a look.

He drew back, raised his hands in mock surren-
der. 'Fine,' he said.

'No. It's *not* fine. You don't say things like that
about my friends.' Her voice was calm, clear and
low. Surprisingly so.

He sighed. 'Stacey. You can say what you like,
but we both know that he's only your friend because
of what he thinks you can get him. And I'd be very
wary, if I were you. Because when things don't go
the way the Borsattos want them to go, they completely lose control. Honey,' he said, extending his
hands onto the table, palms down, 'you're much too
special to be hanging around with someone like him
long term. Sure, right here, right now, he looks good.
He's back in town, building up his profile, running
around with his handsome friend and all the pretty
girls love him. But what can he *really* offer someone
like you, Stacey?'

'I'm going to skip past the part where I tell you
you're a total jerk and cut straight to the main event.
Are you selling the Meadows or not? Because if
you're not, you can kiss me and my "special" ass
goodbye.'

She stood, her hands bunched on the table, and leaned across him.

'I'm merely trying to make you see that you're wasting your time, Stacey. Marco Borsatto is bad news—with or without his precious Sant'Angelo's.'

'Goodbye, Preston. Oh, and if I were you I'd stay well out of the path of the next uncontrollable Borsatto who comes your way. You might just get hurt.'

He laughed. 'Come on—sit back down. Of *course* I'm going to sell the Meadows,' he said as she turned away. 'I just need you to ask me nicely first. Play by the rules.'

'Ask you nicely? Play by the rules? Is that all this is—a *game*?'

She pushed her chair away and began to walk. She didn't know where. But she wasn't going to beg for anyone.

'I'll get the lawyers to draw the papers up tomorrow. Have dinner with me, Stacey? Tomorrow night. Seven o'clock. L'Escargot.'

She couldn't turn around—couldn't stand the sight of him a moment longer. *L'Escargot!* Who did he think he was, bribing her with dinner in the most expensive restaurant in town? As if that mattered a damn.

She headed back through the cocktail lounge. Noël Coward had given way to Adele. The mood was darker, more soulful—a counterpoint to the brash voices and laughter as liquor flowed.

As she moved her heel slid on the polished wooden

floor and she slipped forward. The hem of her dress ripped slightly as she scrabbled to right herself. She was a mess. So much for taking all that time to look elegant. She'd blown her cover, that was for sure. What sort of woman willingly bent over a man's knee and allowed herself to do what they'd done?

And since they had—nothing. Silence. *Why?*

She had to get out of here. Get some air. Figure out her next move. Because one thing was for sure—it wasn't going to be working here for Marco. Not now.

She passed the bathrooms and went in the direction of Marco's suite—one turn and she realised she was heading the wrong way.

Another turn and she was lost.

'It's the long game, man—that's what you've got to play.'

Stacey stopped. She was right outside the fitness suite. The heavy wooden door was ajar. A dim light glowed. She heard a bang and a curse and a sharp intake of breath.

'And maybe find a softer target than the wall or Preston's head.'

'He needs it. He's a worse piece of—'

'Yeah, you've said. And it doesn't help that he's all over your girl. That's got to hurt too.'

'Stacey's not *my* girl. She's *a* girl. Period. She could marry the guy, for all I care. I just want my house back.'

'Sure you do. And tomorrow, when you've slept on it, you'll start back on that path to getting it. But for now—unless you've taken some self-control pills—I suggest you hit the gym before you hit someone for real. I'll go back and tidy up your mess.'

'Do *not* patronise me, Dante. I'll go back and tidy up my own mess.'

'It might have been smarter not to create it in the first place. I get the attraction, but sex in the middle of the business dinner of your life is a bit much even for you.'

'Why don't you shut the hell up? Just back off and mind your own business.'

'Because someone needs to point out the obvious. You're a different person around her. It's like you swallowed some cocktail of jealousy and aggression. And it didn't look like sex as an *entrée* helped calm you down. If anything it worked you up even more.'

'You don't know what you're talking about.'

'I'm talking about you getting whatever she's unleashed back under control. This is *not* how you roll, bud.'

The door slammed open. Stacey jumped back against the wall. Marco walked out, rubbing his knuckles and cursing. Dante walked out behind him and closed the door. Two men who'd turn heads at fifty paces, but Marco had that dark, dangerous edge she'd only seen once before tonight. And that was a night she never wanted to repeat. A night when she'd played her hand and lost.

This time she'd done what she'd thought was the right thing to do. If Marco hadn't got all bent out of shape Preston just might have sold him the thing there and then. But he hadn't. And she had no guarantee that he'd keep his word tomorrow. None at all.

She watched as they made their way back down the corridor and out into the foyer. Then she slipped back out into the hallway, cut along the back of the pool. Off to bed.

Maybe for the last ever time in Montauk.

CHAPTER ELEVEN

MARCO STARED OUT at another clear, bright day and wondered how long he should stay here in the Polo Club, drinking coffee and sending emails that could wait, before he could get on with the matter at hand and start putting things right.

Dante had suggested meeting at eight, going for a ride, maybe hitting a few chukkas. But that had been at three in the morning, half full of beer and bourbon when it had seemed like a good idea. Now, almost four hours later, Marco knew that his energies had to be directed someplace else entirely.

He stretched out his hand to lift his coffee and saw the state of his knuckles from where he'd punched the wall. What a jerk he'd been. What a disaster the whole night had been. And he had nobody but himself to blame.

He should never have allowed that stupid dinner to happen. It had been worse than irresponsible— it had been insane. Not only had he lost any chance of keeping Preston close, and therefore getting the edge on him the way he had intended, he'd completely lost control of himself and had sex with Stacey in a way that had stepped over every boundary he'd ever laid down.

If only she hadn't seemed to invest so much damn *trust* in him. If only it had been a quickie against the wall or on the desk. Hot, fast sex would have been fine. Okay, it might not be dinner etiquette, but at worst they could have got it out of their systems and headed back for the main course.

But, no matter how he tried to reframe it, it *hadn't* just been hot or fast. And it certainly hadn't been meaningless. It had been something else entirely. She had looked at him with that face and those eyes and had taken them both to a place that he hadn't been prepared to go.

And, *dammit*, if it had been anyone else he wouldn't be doing all this soul-searching—but it had been Stacey. He *liked* her—he felt responsible for her. He didn't want to hurt her by letting her think there was going to be any future past the end of today. Stacey Jackson was like a fireworks display. Light it up, stand back and watch. A woman like that would be stimulating, amazing, fun—but totally exhausting.

And trustworthy…?

The jury was still out on that. She was a man's woman, for sure, and that brought its own set of dramas. It had done when she was sixteen and it looked as if she was in for a lifetime of being chased by men.

Not that he was the jealous type. At least he didn't think he was—but watching Preston leer all over her last night had definitely been a factor in his dragging her into the office. At least that was what Dante had said. Several times over the course of last night's analysis.

He lifted the cup and wished he'd asked for an Americano.

'Hey, can I get a long coffee with hot milk this time? Thanks,' he said to the cute blonde waitress who blushed like a red rose and dropped everything every time he so much as looked at her.

She was the very antithesis of the waitress Stacey had been. Stacey had had the whole thing covered—everybody's order, smooth and efficient, but totally contained. As if she didn't give a damn if you had a nice day.

Stacey. He'd tried to be kind and do the right thing when she'd clearly been in a bit of trouble and had had nobody else looking out for her. He'd had no other option but to bring her to Montauk. He couldn't have left her there in Atlantic City, with a concussion and a heavy guy on her tail.

But now it was so messy. He'd need a proper conversation with her later. She could stay on here until her mother got back and then she could start work in one of his other places in town. But they had to draw a line under the sex. It had been a long time coming and it had been amazing. But that was where it ended. This thing was over before it even began.

He drained the coffee. He'd need another two of those at least before he could face more than a single word with anyone. He'd deliberately stayed well out of the way of his suite, sitting up with Dante and the staff as they finished their shifts, had a drink and went home. Finally it had only been the two of them, one foul mood and a whole lot of regret.

'You should go and make sure she's all right,' Dante had said at least five times, his words getting more and more incoherent with each passing beer.

'She's fine,' he'd answered. The last place he'd wanted to be was in her personal space. 'She'll be in bed.'

'You should go and check on her, then. Or at least one of us should.'

At that Marco had roused himself and pulled his head out of the fog he'd sunk under. 'You'll stay well away. There's enough trouble without *you* adding to it.'

'Not sure I follow, but I'll respect your wishes. This time. Only I thought you said she had some kind of head injury?'

Marco had pushed himself to his feet and stomped off through the lounge and back to his suite. He'd known deep down she was well in the clear, but still she was his responsibility, and the last thing he'd wanted was anything to happen to her.

It was only then that he'd realised he wasn't even sure she was still there. She could have cut and run, like she'd done every other time things got a bit too hard to handle. What if she'd actually left with that piece of trash? When he and Dante had made it back to the restaurant the table had been empty, save for a bottle of untouched champagne and a basket of bread rolls. The staff had seen Preston's driver and car, but nobody knew where Stacey had gone.

He'd let it go at that. The last thing he'd wanted to do was go chasing after her.

But those visions of her lying across his desk, of her eyes searching his, had kept slamming into the back of his head. He had been rough, he'd made demands, and he'd loved how she'd complied. He'd never experienced anything like it in his life.

He didn't want to again.

Being with Stacey had always fired up those parts of him that he liked to play down. Cool and calm was how he liked his life. He wasn't like his father—hotheaded and out of control. He didn't have addictions or issues or get into fights. He was nothing like him. Nothing *at all* like him. He'd spent his whole life making sure of it.

He'd climbed the steps up into the suite and pushed open the door.

As silently as his one hundred and eighty pounds would allow he'd crept through to his bedroom—the room where he'd put Stacey when they'd arrived. It had seemed the right thing to do at the time—to hold off what he'd felt sure was inevitable. Maybe if he'd followed his gut instead of his head they wouldn't be in this situation now. But he'd let the tension build to a frenzy, and then what had happened, had happened.

He'd stepped into the room and stilled, listening for the sound of her breathing. Feeling for the sense of her. He'd walked in further and stood by the bed, tuned in to the long soft breaths that had filled the space. Stood there in the darkness.

The winds had picked up during the evening. Roars from the ocean and hard squally blasts had rocked through the town and there had still been remnants at that hour of the morning. But there had been a sense of peace in the room. Despite all the drama and headaches that always seemed to be wrapped up with Stacey Jackson, standing there, listening to the sounds of her in sleep had been soothing.

Strange that he'd found that so reassuring.

He'd stood for a few more moments, then turned around and headed back down to the lounge. Overthinking about women never did anyone any good. He had much more important things to overthink instead.

Stacey's eyes opened onto a golden-tinged day. For a moment she lay, her limbs leaden from a dreamy sleep, her mind frothing with memories of last night. She was still here—that was a first. She rolled over and sat up on one elbow—looked around for signs that Marco had been near.

The door was closed. The room was just as she'd

left it—her clothes packed away, her cosmetics tidy
on the dressing table. The robe that he wore was still
hanging at the side of the en-suite bathroom. He'd
slept in another bedroom the first night, but she'd
thought after what they'd done that he might end up
waking her in the night.

The fact that he hadn't hurt a little, she realised.
More than a little. Like holding a hot coal against
her chest, she felt it burn. She'd felt the pain of rejection before—felt it more sore and harder than now.
But she was ready for it this time—and she wasn't
going to let it get any hotter, cause any more blisters on her heart.

So, much as she was tempted to curl up under the
sheet and relive those moments in his office, it would
be about the stupidest thing she could do. What she
needed to do was work out the smart thing to do.

Every other time it had involved moving on. This
time she'd been going to give it a shot, hang out a little longer. But was that *really* the smart thing to do?
Or should she chalk yet another one down to experience and head off someplace totally fresh?

'Hi.'

She jerked her head up. Marco. Standing in the
doorway.

'Hi,' she said.

'I brought you coffee.'

He walked towards her, same old gorgeous Marco,
but forever changed to her now. He set the coffee
down on the table beside the bed.

'How are you feeling?' he asked, sitting on the edge of the bed.

She was wearing a slip nightdress, and she was covered by a sheet, but she felt exposed despite what they'd shared. She drew her knees up to her chin.

'I'll get back to you on that. After the coffee,' she said, reaching for it. 'Thanks. How about you?'

'Now? I feel pretty good. Last night? Less so. We need to talk about what happened, Stacey.'

She sipped the coffee and put it down.

'Happy to.'

She sat up properly. The sheet fell away from her. The spaghetti straps of the nightdress and the deep-sliced neckline held very little cover. Marco glanced and then turned his head. Very deliberately.

So that was how it was going to be. He couldn't have painted his regret any more vividly. She felt a prickle of fight. 'Are you starting with an apology?'

He turned back to face her. 'I'm sorry about the whole thing. It was a mess. From start to finish.'

She thought about that for a minute. Then she swung her legs out from under the covers and stood.

'That's it? That's your apology? *I'm sorry it was a mess?* Doesn't cut it, Marco. Not from where I'm standing.'

She put her hands on her hips and waited.

'*And* I'm sorry about walking out on you the way I did. That's not how I normally handle things. It was juvenile.'

He stood too. She looked more closely. He was

fresh, scrubbed clean and handsome as the day was long. But he still had that barbed, tense air and the low thrum of menace. He was still a man on edge, despite what he wanted her to think.

She swallowed. Didn't matter a damn. He'd been out of line too many times now.

'It was way past juvenile. It was messed up. Humiliating. Weird. Actually, it was just weird.'

'I wouldn't describe it as that. You seemed to be into it as much as I was.'

She did a double take. She hadn't expected that.

'Are we talking about the sex, here?' No way was he going to brush things under the carpet. 'I was talking about your behaviour being weird. The sex is a whole other conversation.'

'Well, let's have it. No point in putting it off.'

He looked angry. Again.

Stacey felt her heart quicken. Felt a rush of stress whoosh through her body. Anxiety gripped her in that way it did when she was confronted with something she didn't like—and the only way out was to fight or run.

'It was—' she began.

'The timing was wrong and it was a bit out of left field. Is that what you're trying to say? But it wasn't weird. Not in my opinion.'

He stared at her, then seemed to shake his head in disgust. Or maybe incredulity.

'I'm going to start again, Stacey. The whole thing was a mistake and a mess. My business life is my own. I never mix business with pleasure, and last night I let not one but two barriers down. I'm sorry if that's hard to hear, but it's the only thing I can say.'

'You can say anything you like. You can say, *Hey I made a fool of myself, I made a fool of you, I let myself down*—you can say all those things. But you're choosing to say you don't like to mix business with pleasure. Well, good for you. At least you have *one* bit of self-knowledge.'

She walked past him to reach for his robe. She wanted cover. She wanted to wrap herself up and tell him what she'd done for him. She wanted his self-knowledge to extend to seeing it from *her* point of view.

All she'd tried to do was keep the conversation going so that he could get Preston to accept his stupid offer. Did he think she'd really *wanted* to sit opposite yet another man who groped her body with his eyes, who patronised her and denigrated her just because he was a man, and a wealthy man at that. Had he *any* idea what it had cost her to do that?

'What's that supposed to mean?'

'Doesn't matter,' she said quietly. 'I won't be hanging around for an apology. I've decided I'm heading to New York later today.'

It was as if last night's storm had suddenly returned, but worse. A silent storm. Breathless and violent.

'You're supposed to be waiting to see your mother.'

'For the record, I moved away from home ten

years ago. I've had worse things happen to me than a bump on the head, and I've never once come running home to my mother. That was all *your* doing. I don't like it here. Do you understand? That's why I don't visit. I. Don't. Want. To. Be. Here.'

'I see.'

She let her hand hang in mid-air beside his robe. There wasn't going to be time for a leisurely goodbye. No time for a shower—no morning-after sex. No *Let's see where this thing goes with us* conversation. He'd made that perfectly clear. She'd pack and go now.

She turned back round to face him. 'Marco—let's not pretend that you want me around. You hold me responsible for the disaster with Preston. You probably hold me responsible for what happened in your office. And for the polar ice caps melting and everything else that's wrong with the world. It's like your whole life was on track until you bumped into *me*.'

'I had *one thing* left I wanted to accomplish—that's all.'

'Sure. Good for you. I'll get out of your hair and let you get on with accomplishing it.'

'You mean you're going to run off again? We should talk this thing through, Stacey. That would be the mature thing to do.'

She stopped pulling underwear out of the drawer, where the overconfident maid had packed it away, and started to stuff it into her bag.

'Oh, get over yourself. You're *so* mature—I get it.

You're *so* sorted—you never do anything wrong, do you? Is that because you never do *anything*, period? You never take risks in case—oh, I don't know—in case things go wrong and something slips out of control. And, hey, you might *just* find out that you're a hell of a lot more like your father than you think you are!'

The words were out—they had flown out of her mouth and landed like daggers on the floor. She hadn't even known what was coming, but there they were—gleaming and deadly—and there was no way of getting them back.

'I've told you before—my personal life and my business life are my own.'

His voice was frozen. She longed to be able to claw something back but he'd closed down. She watched him recoil from her. She longed to go to him but he was in total lockdown. Back in complete control. Nothing ruffling him, nothing moving him to anything more than the twitch of a muscle in his jaw.

And watching him like that made her more and more wild. More and more angry that he could just disregard what she'd done for him—what they'd done together. She'd bared more than her flesh for him—she'd trusted him not to hurt her.

But he didn't give a damn about anything other than his wretched family jewels and his reputation. He wouldn't even give a damn that she'd stood up for him and his family with Preston. She'd had his back but what point would there be in telling him *that*?

She picked up those knives and stuck them in further.

'You don't have a personal life in Montauk, Marco. You know that better than anyone—so why are you pretending? Everyone knows that your mother had addiction issues and your father gambled it all away. You think they're not all sitting on their porches wondering if you'll go the same way? Do you think that every single detail of what happened here last night won't have been swapped in the bars and along the beach and at the harbour? Come on—you've not forgotten that much, have you? *Hotshot Borsatto and the Town Tramp!* This morning's headlines.'

'You're really going for it this time, Stacey, but I'm not rising to your bait. I came here to apologise. I thought we could get over what we did. But I'm not getting involved in your acid.'

'If I'm spitting acid it's because of you and this place. The moment I stepped back in I remembered why I'd left.'

'Well, I'm sorry you feel that way. It could have turned out differently.'

'Could it? *How?* You're clearly regretting bringing me here. Or are you just regretting the fact that we had sex?'

She turned then, to face him. She wasn't afraid of him. Standing there like a hurricane ready to blow.

'I didn't say I regretted it. I just don't want you to read more into it than it was.'

'What *was* it?'

His darkly lashed eyes were trained straight onto hers. His brow furrowed and his mouth pursed.

'It *should* have been fun. A one-time thing. A quickie, for God's sake. But it wasn't. It was intense. And it can't happen again.'

'I don't think it was any big deal. I've had better. So don't bother having a conscience about anything that happened. It happened. Move on. Preston might sell you your damned house back. If he doesn't— so what? You can buy another. And you can fill it full of people with class and money. Yeah, and girls who will be mature the morning after—no questions asked. I'm sure they're choking up the highway trying to get here already.'

His face now was rigid as Rushmore. Stern and disparaging. Her childhood friend stood before her, hating her. But that was no surprise, really. It had only ever been a matter of time before he joined the ranks.

'I think I'd say your head injury is not an issue any more. As soon as you've packed there'll be a car waiting to take you to your mother's. Goodbye, Stacey.'

He turned and walked to the door. The handful of silk she held crushed in her hand slid and fell at her feet. He moved through the door and she braced herself for the bang. But it didn't come. He closed it as quietly and carefully as if there was a baby sleeping. She watched the handle move back up as he released it on the other side and then she heard the almost silent tread of his feet as he moved off down the hall.

In the mirror beside the dressing table she saw herself reflected. Pale, hunched and drawn. The nightdress, a mirror of silvery satin, hugged her body, traced her shape, outlined where he'd touched her and seemed to rejoice in her. He'd grasped her hips and palmed her breasts. He'd kissed her and lifted her and poured himself into her.

She'd always wondered what loving him would be like. She'd always wanted him. And finally having him had been wilder and better than anything she'd ever known. But losing him as a friend was a worse pain than she could ever imagine.

She lifted the silk robe at her feet and held it out. She used it to dab at the tears that rolled down her face. Tears seeped from her eyes and poured freely. Silently. Achingly.

What had she done? *What had she done?*

She'd handled it so badly—again. His emotions were high…he'd lost his deal. She could have tried to see it from his point of view. Maybe if she'd let him talk it through he'd have felt better about what they'd done. She'd been such a good listener in the past—he'd told her so. But when the listening was about her she couldn't handle it. She knew that.

She sat on the bed, curled in on herself and slid to the ground as one wrenching, silent sob racked her after another. Then she bunched the silk around her hand and stuffed her fist in her mouth to stop the howl that was building inside.

When was she going to stop fighting the world?

You're going to be a lonely, bitter old woman.

Across the floor the mirror told her the ugly truth. She was lonelier and more bitter than she could ever have thought possible. She had nothing. No friends, no job, no lover. No family apart from her mother, whom she'd avoided for years.

And she was exhausted.

For an hour she lay there, curled up. Finally her breathing eased…her eyes began to open. She had to get herself up. She had to go.

Feeling greyer than the thick veil of clouds wrapped over the sky, she showered, dressed and tied up her hair.

She left the luggage, the clothes, the cosmetics and the jewellery. She wore the simplest outfit—leggings and a sweater.

She made her way through the suite and down the hallway. Out through Reception. She looked around to see if she could see him. She'd steadied herself enough to be able to say, *Goodbye, so long, no hard feelings* if he was there—but he wasn't. There was no sign. Just some little blonde waitress with rosy cheeks, pouring coffee and looking fresh and carefree, the way she herself must have once looked.

She walked over to her. 'Tell your boss the coast's clear,' she said to her startled face. And then she stopped. 'Sorry—I didn't mean to snap. I'd appreciate if you could pass that on. Thanks.'

She stepped out to the entrance, where cars were being dropped for valet parking. Good as his word, there was a car waiting. She slid in and tugged the door closed.

'Get me as far away from this place as you can, driver.'

The engine turned over and they were off.

CHAPTER TWELVE

MARCO PULLED HARD on the reins and the pony spun to a stop. He rattled the ball as far up the field as he could and saw it clear the goal mouth.

A cheer came up from the stablehands, who had stopped work to watch the electrifying match between their two bosses—one of whom was a professional player, the other the best amateur on the circuit—but it barely registered with him. A momentary lapse in his black mood was all.

'I've had enough,' he called to Dante, indicating with a slash of his hand through the air that he was out of there. They could get someone to replace him—there were enough eager players from among the youngsters at Dante's Polo Foundation to fill another four teams.

Dante saluted with his stick and sent him one of his golden smiles. To the world that guy was the luckiest, easiest, happiest man on the planet. Only Marco knew differently. For all his light there were dark, deep shadows. And it was the shadows that made him the best friend and confidant any man could ask for. Dante had lived more than anyone knew, buried more than anyone could stomach, and for that Marco treasured his advice. But right now he didn't want to hear it.

Right now he had other things to be getting on with.

He passed his pony to one of the kids and headed for a shower. It was another hour until the dinner Dante had arranged at Betty's. A whole load of the old crowd were going to be there, plus a whole load of the new crowd. Dante was well connected—too well connected. Marco had tried to tell him that after the weekend he'd had the last thing he wanted was a party, but he'd said Montauk was turning into a party town and, anyway, it might do him good to socialise.

He began to make his way through the club to his suite. He really should look at moving in to the villa he'd bought along the coast. He'd never really seen himself moving back into the sprawling buildings of Sant'Angelo's anyway. It never had been about recreating his childhood home—it was more about getting back what was his: the Borsatto estate, Sant'Angelo's. But Stacey was right. The fact that the locals still called it by a name from the mists of time really made him think. Who was he actually fighting this fight *for*?

He needed a base here, and while it had been great using this place while he and Dante had been kicking the whole Polo Club and Foundation off, it was a thriving business now and didn't need his oversight in any way. The management were extremely capable.

And he'd been about to add Stacey to that group. At least he could be grateful that *that* hadn't happened.

He paused at the reception desk to check for messages. There was only one for him. From Ms Jackson, to say that 'the coast was clear'. The girl on the desk paused, dipped her head. Told him that another message had come in for Ms Jackson herself, after she'd left. From Mr Chisholm. To say that he would send his car at six-forty-five for their dinner reservation. Would Mr Borsatto pass that on to her? Or should she contact Mr Chisholm to say there seemed to be a misunderstanding since Ms Jackson wasn't here?

Marco almost choked.

What dinner reservation? The normally unflappable reception manager looked horrified. She apologised and said that she really didn't know. Would he like her to find out more?

Marco growled some kind of answer and headed off to his suite. Dinner reservation? With Preston? She wasn't *seriously* thinking she could continue where she'd left off? Why was she staging a repeat of last night—involving herself even more in his business? Surely she wasn't actually going for *dinner* with the guy?

He threw open the door and strode into the suite.

He'd half expected she might still be there, and the lurch in his stomach when she wasn't was relief—it really was.

He marched into the en-suite bathroom and fired on the shower, hauled his T-shirt over his head and shoved down his jeans. He was *this* close to punching the wall again. But there was only one finger he definitely *hadn't* broken after his fight with the wall the night before, and the pain in the others even from holding the reins held him in check—just.

He soaped himself and rinsed himself and stepped out to dry himself—and it was only then that he noticed all the stuff lying around. Dragging the towel across his chest, he walked over to the dressing table and saw all the little bottles that were still arranged there. Two black pearl earrings caught his eye. He lifted them and rolled them around his palm, observing their luminescence. Maybe she'd left in a hurry and not noticed them? Or maybe Preston had promised her better-quality ones at his house…?

He dried his back and his face and tossed the towel down in the laundry basket—and there he saw a piece of lingerie…the slip that he'd bought her. And then, when he walked into the dressing room, he saw all the pieces of luggage. He hauled them over and sprang open the brass locks. Inside was every garment he'd bought her.

He shoved his hands in and pulled them out, scattered them all over the floor.

Damn her. She'd gone and she was still driving

him mad. It was like the last time. He'd totally lost control and been thrown off his own land back then but it had been because of her that he'd been down in the summerhouse at all. Trying to stay the hell away from the world. Calm down.

Well, this ended *now*.

He threw on his clothes and stuffed all her clothes back inside the luggage. It was a petty, stupid gesture to leave them all there. What kind of woman *did* that?

One who had learned that there was plenty more where that came from.

So she was having dinner with Chisholm. You couldn't make it up!

He grabbed everything up, picked up his keys and strode off down the hall and out into the warmth of the early evening. His car was at the back but the valet had it there in seconds. All the staff were looking at him as if he was some kind of monster. They kept their heads down and made no eye contact, but he could tell they were keeping well back. And that was needling him as well.

He was never like this. *Never!* He was calm, smooth and totally in control. He was measured in the way he approached every aspect of his life. Always the same way. That was how he wanted to be known—and he was. He was as far removed as a hot-headed Italian as it was possible to be.

Until that woman came anywhere near him!

He threw the luggage across the back seat and got

in the driver's seat. In minutes he was at the edge of the estate. In another ten he'd be at Chisholm's. One minute after that he'd have dumped every last shred of her stuff onto Chisholm's driveway—and if he saw the guy this time he really *would* rip his head off.

After that he was going to get back in the car and head round to Betty's. He didn't need this kind of hassle in his life. He needed to put Sant'Angelo's and Stacey Jackson behind him and he needed to do that *now*.

He got to Chisholm's driveway just as the gates were opening to allow a car out. He was in it. Marco screeched his car to a stop in front of it and jumped out. Two strides and he was at his door, yanking it open before his driver had even realised what had happened.

'What's going on, Borsatto? You got what you wanted, didn't you?'

'Get out!' Marco yelled, reaching inside the limousine to drag at Preston.

'Get your hands off me or I'll change my mind, you maniac. What the hell are you doing?'

'Where is she? I've got her stuff. Tell her—get her here now and tell her.'

'Have you lost your mind? I accepted your offer and now I'm heading out to meet Stacey for dinner. At least *someone* knows how to say thank you.'

Marco put his hands on Preston's collar and heaved him right out of the car. He flung him up against the side of the limo and drew his hand back.

'You touch me and it's all off. I swear, Borsatto. I only signed those papers because of her. You lay a finger on me and I rip the whole thing up.'

Marco dropped his fist. Dropped the arm he'd been holding him with. He took two steps back and shoved his palm to his forehead.

'What are you talking about?'

His voice was quiet. He could hardly speak for the strain in his throat.

'What do you *think* I'm talking about? You and your damn house. Stacey called me today and convinced me that I should accept your offer. What the hell are you looking at me like that for? I don't give a damn about your run-down dump. You can have it with my blessing. One less headache, as far as I'm concerned. Now, get the hell out of my road. I don't want to be late.'

Marco stepped back and watched as Preston got back in his car and disappeared in a cloud of dusty gravel.

He'd heard the words but he couldn't quite process them. He reached for his phone. He had to find out what had happened. He punched in his code. Called the Polo Club. Told them to find the driver who had driven Stacey. He wanted to know exactly where she'd gone. And he wanted someone to look out for Preston's car. And for them to phone him straight back if Stacey Jackson appeared. Not to let her leave the club if she showed up.

Maybe she'd gone to stay at her mother's and was

going to meet Preston at the club? Maybe she'd taken an apartment in town.

Maybe. But it didn't feel like any of that. She was gone. He could sense it. In the empty howl of the wind. In the grey drops of rain that landed like lonely confetti all around. In the quiet, lifeless land that witnessed…waited.

He drove on along the coastline. He passed people on bikes, families, couples. He saw a figure off in the distance. He strained to see if it was a brunette with long legs and a crazy, giving heart.

Whatever and wherever she was, he had to hear this story from her lips. It didn't add up. Preston had signed over Sant'Angelo's?

He called his realtor. Saturday night it might be, but that was what he paid him for.

Sure enough. The offer had been accepted in principle.

His phone rang. Dante.

'Hey, man, we're waiting for you. What's the hold-up?'

'I've just found out that Preston has agreed to sell. The deal's gone through.'

Dante's holler sounded out in the car and it was only then that Marco realised what he'd actually just said.

'Amazing! Where are you? Are you headed to Betty's? We'll see you here in—how long are you going to be?'

'I'm on my way. I want to swing by the Jackson place first.'

There was a pause, and then Dante filled it. 'Sure. Good idea. Okay, well… See you when you get here. Tell us about it then.'

Marco knew as he swung his car down the sandy road to Stacey's mom's house that she wasn't going to be there. He parked the car and got out. Walked past her neighbours' houses. A beat-up car and some bits of junk. Sand and tufts of grass.

Their house was right at the end.

The path was neat, and there were little tubs of flowers. Paintwork was fresh. Marilyn Jane had always tried to put on a good show. He remembered that. Appearances meant a lot to her.

He passed the swing that creaked in the breeze, walked to the door and knocked.

Nothing.

CHAPTER THIRTEEN

FOR DAYS THE rain had been incessant, and now the whole place was a pallet of green. The air, heavy and succulent, hummed with the vigorous growth that only happened in the wet warmth of late spring. Some folks were glad, and some were counting the minutes until it dried up. But as the train pulled into Montauk station the sun finally dazzled through the clouds and beamed an inverted rainbow smile down on everyone.

Stacey pulled her windcheater tightly round her shoulders and waited. One week later than arranged, her mom was finally heading back from Canada. The call they'd shared when Stacey had been on the train to NYC had been tense, but she'd promised her mother faithfully that she'd return within the week. And she'd meant every word.

In between times she'd *had* to get out of Montauk. Staying there while Marco pounded through her head and her heart was not an option.

Was she naïve? Or just plain stupid? Either way,

a few days in Manhattan to clear her head and serve up the epiphany she needed to figure out her next move hadn't worked.

At least she had the money to have choices. Whatever Marco had done to Bruce, her back-pay from Decker's and a whole load more had wound up in her bank account.

So now here she was, three years since her last farewell to her mother, at this very station, as good as her word. She looked along the platform. The old guy from the tuna place tipped his hat and smiled. She smiled back. The couple who ran the craft store that her mom had taken her to as soon as she could walk were there, waiting to pick up their granddaughter. Sweet people. She'd chatted to them when she'd arrived back a few days earlier and now she smiled them another greeting. Along the road, taxis queued, and she'd paused already to talk to a driver who'd called out to her, one arm hanging out of his window, shooting the breeze about their school days.

People began to exit the train and she strained to see her mother.

'Stacey. Honey.'

She looked up.

'Mom—*wow.*'

Her mother stepped towards her and hugged her in a warm embrace. Stacey buried her nose in the thick hair so like hers. She breathed her in and closed her eyes. Together they rocked backwards and forwards while she relearned her mother's shape, felt her warmth, her bones, her love.

'Let me look at you, baby girl.'

Stacey stepped back and let her mother smooth her hair and stare at her in that dazed eyed, proud way she always did. But if anyone was dazed it was Stacey.

'Mom—I can't believe—you look amazing. So—*young*!'

Her mother laughed. A vibrant, rich laugh. Her eyes sparkled.

'What's going on? Are you in love?' asked Stacey warily.

This wasn't how it was supposed to be. It was supposed to be the daughter all sparkly and lovestruck—not the mom.

They walked along the platform arm in arm. It was the strangest thing. Men stared and women stared. Their eyes flicked from her to her mom. Admiration and interest. No mistake. And no wonder.

'Well, *are* you? With this guy from Toronto? Tell me about him.'

'First things first. How is your poor head? And your leg? Are you sure you're all right? Marco was so worried.'

'Let's knock *that* on the head, Mom. Marco was worried I was going to file a claim against him. Marco is not the guy you remember, I'm sorry to say.'

She felt her mother's hand on her arm, felt a soft squeeze.

'Oh, dear. Did those fireworks explode again?'

'What are you talking about?'

'You two couldn't breathe the same air without there being some kind of explosion. You're both so passionate. Totally made for one another.'

'I know you like him, Mom, but he's not the guy for me. I can hardly stand to breathe the same air as him now. I mean, don't get me wrong—he was kind, I suppose. He got me checked out. Twice, in fact. And he got these two guys to come from a mall in Atlantic City—bought me everything I could need. Stuff I could never afford. Dresses, jeans, sweaters—you name it. But it was all him playing a part. None of it was real.'

'I don't know about any of that, but he called me—that was real—and I'm so grateful to him,' her mother cut in. 'That was the right thing to do. And he promised me he would take good care of you.'

They walked along the line of cars that prowled outside the station. People jostled them, going this way and that.

'Yeah, he did.'

He did take good care of me, she thought, suddenly remembering him with the paramedics, in the car, checking on her when he thought she was sleeping that first night at the Polo Club. Remembering waking up in his arms when she'd fainted and seeing the look in his eyes.

She swallowed. Her eyes burned.

'So, tell me about Toronto guy,' she said, changing

the subject and squeezing her mom's hand. 'What's his name? How long you been seeing him?'

Her mom smiled.

'His name is John. And I've been seeing him these past two years. I spend a lot of time in Canada. Mostly all the time now, if I'm honest. We're getting married, honey.'

Stacey stared. Looked at her. Properly looked at her. Her mother *couldn't* be having a relationship. She'd spent her entire life burning a candle for her husband.

'Two years? You've been dating for *two years*? But what about Dad?'

'What about him? I gave him an ultimatum. He left. We got divorced. That's all history, sweetheart.'

'*You* gave *him* an ultimatum? But I thought— That's not what happened. He left us to be with another woman.'

'He left us because I told him to go. You were so young—you didn't understand. I didn't want you getting caught up in the fall-out of our relationship. Maybe I was overprotective, too careful with the truth, but I don't hold with adults using their children as weapons. And you were, and still are, my whole world.'

Stacey looked around. People moved past them in a blur. In her mind the house of cards upon which her whole miserable childhood had been built began to collapse. Images cracked and split.

Her dad ruffling her hair—for the last time. Say-

ing goodbye. *'You've got to love yourself before anyone else will love you.'*

All this time she'd thought he was telling her she
was unlovable—but had he been talking about himself?

Her mother wringing her hands and closing the
door. She'd been lonely, but she was strong. She'd
protected her this whole time.

'But you were so sad. You ran up all that debt...'

'Stacey, I wasn't so sad after a while. You just
didn't know it because you were away so long. I had
to make a life for myself so I started a little business,
honey. I was making soft furnishings, just like I always wanted, and I opened a shop. But the timing
was wrong. I lost a lot of money, yes, but there was
no need for *you* to step in and take over. I was on top
of things but you wouldn't listen—you never did.'

Stacey stared around as the crowds dispersed. She
couldn't take it all in. Her mother was talking as if she
was sorted and strong. She wasn't a weak, anxiety-
ridden dishcloth after all. How could she have called
it so wrong?

But she had. She'd had her father up on a pedestal
right up until the day she'd seen with her own eyes
that he'd moved on with his new family.

Her mother had never bad-mouthed him. Never
maligned him. She'd let her make up her own mind
about him. She'd protected Stacey as best she could.
And all that anger at living in a broken home on the
wrong side of the tracks—all that anger at herself

for being the cause of it... Anger was a mask for grief. And grief was what she'd felt at having her little world pulled apart.

'I'd love you to meet John soon, yes? How do you feel about that? I know he's not your father, and I'm sorry I couldn't make that work for you. But it was better that he left, honey. I didn't want you growing up thinking that what we had was good, or even normal. It was better that we all had a chance of a better life.'

Marilyn hugged her hard and Stacey gulped down a sob.

'We only get one life, Stacey. You have to find what's right for you and go right on out there and make it happen.'

Marco poured out the third bottle of champagne and upended it in the ice bucket.

'Another?' Dante asked, his eyebrow hitching up.

'Why not?' said Marco. 'Everyone seems to be enjoying themselves.'

He looked along the length of the table. He knew maybe half the faces. He'd be happy if he never saw half of them again. But it was Saturday night. Party night. The night of his big celebration. He'd waited the best part of ten years for this, and now that it was here he was going to do what the world expected and damn well enjoy himself.

Last Saturday the thought of celebrating had been the furthest thing from his mind. He'd driven away

from the Jackson place straight to the airstrip and he-
licoptered out. He'd punished his body and swamped
his mind so that he couldn't even stop to think of
what had happened. International businesses came in
handy when you needed them, and he'd flown out to
the gold fields in India, where it had all started, then
to the Borsatto vineyards in Italy, the cattle farms of
Brazil, and then back to the States to attend this party
that Dante was so determined he was going to have.

He was exhausted. And damn happy.

A slender redhead that he vaguely remembered
from some party in New York—a photographer, or
something in advertising…he couldn't remember
which—looked as if she wanted a private party later
on.

He looked her up and down. For a moment. She
was very pretty, vivacious. Everyone seemed to like
her. And he was totally uninterested.

'I don't think *everyone's* enjoying themselves, no,'
said Dante. 'Not yet, at least.' He nodded at the redhead. 'Interested? Would *that* raise a smile?'

'Not my type,' said Marco, turning his back and
checking his phone again. No calls, no messages. He
slipped it back in his pocket.

Dante laughed. 'No kidding?' he said. 'Though
on the plus side at least you know you have a *type*
now. That's progress.'

Marco reached for a beer and took a long, deep
drink. Dante had let the whole thing lie. Until now.
But he could feel it bubbling to the surface. And he

wasn't ready to go there. Bile began to rise in his throat.

'Heard anything?' asked Dante.

He took another swig. *Here it came.*

'Nope,' he said, folding his arms across his body and resting the beer bottle at the crook of his elbow.

He looked around again. Same old gingham-clothed tables, same old wooden furniture, same old Betty's. Locals, visitors, nobodies and people who thought they were somebodies. He'd got a buzz out of this place for years, but tonight the magic just didn't seem to be working.

'Are you going to leave it at that?'

'Absolutely. Who needs all that drama in their life?'

'Marco, what exactly are we talking about, here?'

He took another swig. It was beginning to make him feel sick.

'We're talking about me feeling normal—whatever that is—for the first time since I saw her bringing the whole of Atlantic City to a halt. We're *talking*, since you're asking, about me waking up in the morning on Planet Earth and *not* being caught up in the intergalactic tailspin of *that* woman. I might have flown right round the world in less than a week, but now I finally get to feel grounded.'

'Ah. Right. You mean Stacey. I get it.'

Marco turned around, felt his jaw tense and his teeth ache even more than they did already.

'What did you *think* we were talking about?'

Dante looked past his shoulder. He beamed one of his big stupid grins and winked at someone. Marco bunched his fists.

'Dial it down, man,' said Dante. 'I thought we were talking about the architects' drawings for your house. I thought since that's always been your life's ambition you would be keen to get it all signed off and the work started. But I get it—I do. Partying is important. And having your life back the way you want it is important too.'

'Damn right it is.'

'Yeah, it's going to be great when it's all finished. What size is the place again? Biggest house on Long Island, right? You're going to have such a *great* time there. No one to bother you. You can have parties every night in different rooms. All the girls. Gonna be amazing.'

'Yeah.'

'Yeah…'

They stood in Betty's, silently swigging their beers, staring at the crowd of girls who always followed them. Really attractive girls—models, actresses, singers. Marco scanned the faces that were turned to them like a field of sunflowers. Expectant, waiting for him to go over and strike up conversation. Waiting for ever.

'Yeah. Bachelor's paradise.'

'Totally.'

'Bet you can't wait to get started.'

'Counting down the seconds.'

'What's holding you back, then? Have you had a look in here tonight?'

Marco put his beer down carefully. He wasn't stupid. He knew exactly what Dante was up to. 'Go on. Spit it out.'

'Okay. Seems to me that your ten-year wait wasn't so much about a house as about a woman.'

'I was *not* burning a candle for Stacey Jackson. It was luck that had her landing on my car. *Bad* luck. If I'd never seen her again I couldn't have cared less.'

'You call that bad luck? You've just had the biggest piece of real estate fall in your lap, courtesy of *her*. Even more—it was *Borsatto* real estate. That's huge—immense. Anyone in your shoes should be dancing on the table right now, but you're crying into your beer over your *bad luck*?'

'I'm not crying into my beer at all. I'm having a *great* time.'

'My mistake. But it looks to me like you're angry with the world.'

'You don't know what you're talking about.'

'I know that I never saw you act the way you did around a woman the way you did around her last week. I've never seen any woman affect you the way she did. It was quite something.'

'If I was acting weird it was stress. Over the deal.'

'Was it? Looked a hell of a lot more like jealousy to me—but maybe that was the angle I was sitting at.'

'I don't have a jealous bone in my body. I made

sure *that* got amputated the last time she made a fool of me.'

'Ah…' Dante chuckled and turned himself right around. He nodded his head slowly and a big smile crept over his face.

Marco, his eyes still trained on the party, observed him from the corner of his eye.

'Right. She made a fool of you. *She* made a fool of *you*?'

Marco swallowed down on the ball of anger that lodged in his chest. 'Yeah—when we were kids. She made a damn fool of me. And I *respected* her!'

He could hear his voice rise. He had to get a handle on himself. Just the mention of her name and he could feel his blood surge.

He took a breath, quietened his voice. 'I set myself boundaries with her because I thought she was—special. All the time she was playing me for a fool. There were other guys… It doesn't matter now.'

'Seems like it matters a hell of a lot. You sound sore, man.'

'I'm not sore. Just disappointed. I mean I *was* disappointed—back then. All I could think was what did they have that I didn't? Was it because I'd lost all my money? I thought she was the one person who really didn't give a damn. About money or cars or land or houses or any of that. Turned out I was wrong. And I still haven't figured out what was in it for her this time around—getting Chisholm to sell. But there *has* to have been some kind of payback.'

'I don't know either, but now is your chance to find out. Why don't you ask her?'

Marco twisted his head to follow the direction of Dante's gaze. He looked down the length of the table—ice buckets, wine and water glasses, bottles of beer and bourbon, baskets of fried chicken and crab claws, French fries and bread, girls and boys and smiles and laughter—and there, at the end, high-lighted in the doorway, tall and proud and beautiful, stood Stacey.

The carnival atmosphere was soon replaced by a series of nudges and whispers and faces turning this way and that. Marco turned to face her. Dante lifted his arm to her in a wave, blew her a kiss and then beckoned a welcome.

Stacey stood. She didn't move. She just looked at every one of the faces in turn and finally at Marco.

Then she stepped into the room—away from the frame that the door had lent her. She walked as she always did. A slow prowl, her chin dipped and the haughty air. She paused for a moment as she neared their table.

Marco saw that down at the end of the table were a whole bunch of people she probably knew. Girls from school. He'd seen this scene before.

'Easy does it,' he said under his breath.

He watched as she trained her eyes along the twin rows of faces, a half-smile playing at her lips, until finally she got to him.

He took a step towards her.

'Good luck,' he heard Dante whisper from behind him.

She continued her prowl, right up to him, and then stopped.

'Party, Marco?' she said, the little smile widening as she cast her arm out in a gesture towards the clutter of their celebration.

'Thanks to you. Yes.'

She made a face as if to say, *You're welcome.* 'So the deal went through after all?'

Marco nodded. 'Yes. It's incredible. And at the price I offered. I still can't believe it.'

'Good. I'm happy for you.'

'Stacey?'

'What?' she said, gazing at him.

She looked different. It was exactly a week since he'd left her in his suite, standing there in her silk nightdress, looking at him with those eyes, expecting more than he could offer.

'We need to talk.'

She didn't look as if she felt much like talking.

He tried again. 'Let's get out of here.'

'And leave your party? When you're all having such *fun*?'

He looked over her shoulder. People were getting on with it. The redhead was flitting about, camera in hand. So she *was* a photographer after all.

'I didn't come here to join your party. So, no—thanks all the same. Hi, there, Dante,' she said as he raised his hand at her, beamed and then turned himself away and got on with his drink.

'I see. But you came back at least. It's good to see you.'

She continued to ignore him, instead glancing round at the faces who looked back at her.

'That's quite the A-list crowd you've got following you now.'

'I couldn't give a damn about them, Stacey. Where did you go?'

'After you ordered me to leave, you mean?' She swivelled her head back to face him. 'Where did I go? I left.'

Marco stared at that face. Her eyes gave nothing away. *Nothing.* They were just two indigo pools. She blinked and continued to look at him. She was being deliberately belligerent. And he was struck by the need to kiss it right out of her.

The spark that always flared between them ignited with sudden force. He wanted her in the way he knew he always would. He wanted to taste her and touch her and feel her soft, hot flesh under his. He wanted to hold her very essence in his hands and make her submit to him. Over and over.

He reached out and put his fingers around her elbow, tugged her towards him.

She held on to the back of the chair she stood beside and refused to budge. Her jaw tightened and her eyes suddenly flashed to life.

'I want to talk to you,' he said.

'I can't think what there is left to say.'

'Stacey, we have a lot to discuss, and I would like to do it in private.'

'I'm sure you would,' she said. 'But you had your chance. Anyway, I'm not here to see you.'

She turned her head, as if looking for someone.

'Are you here on a *date*?'

He spun round, looking. There were guys everywhere—staring at her. Despite the fact that there were two Hollywood actresses and at least one *Vogue* cover girl, Stacey Jackson pulled more looks than all of them.

'You really are incredibly insecure around me, aren't you?' she said, shaking her head and laughing.

Marco felt the last bubble of self-restraint pop in his head. The passion she brought out in him overflowed. She shouldn't be acting like this.

'You still haven't learned any manners.'

'You've probably got a point there, but *you're* the last person I'd go to for lessons.'

He leaned in closer, aware of the interest of the people close at hand.

'You know that if this wasn't such a public place I'd throw you over my shoulder and march you outside—take you somewhere to *really* teach you respect.'

Her lashes swept closed for a moment, and he was struck by the incredible beauty of the line of each eye. But when she opened them to him they were filled with the fire he knew so well.

'You've tried that. All you taught me was a little bit more about myself. And a lot more about *you*.'

He stepped closer again. He was ablaze with the need to touch her. She was like some kind of life-blood he had to feel flowing through his veins. She was everything he wanted in a woman. Whatever deal she'd struck with Preston, he'd knock it out of the park.

He gripped her jaw—didn't give a damn who was watching now. He let his fingers caress her skin, his thumb stroke her lip.

'What's that supposed to mean?' he asked.

She put her hand on his. 'We have the most amazing sexual chemistry. We could have taken it further—that's all I'm saying.'

She turned her head into the palm of his hand as it still held her cheek. She pressed a kiss against his hand, closed her eyes.

'What are you talking about—*could* have?' He pulled his hand from her face, circled her arm and tugged her closer still.

At that she seemed to puff herself up.

'*Could* have. It's not that hard to understand.'

'Stacey. Whatever you want—'

He looked around. The beaming flower faces were still mostly trained in their direction. Dante had sat down and was deep in conversation with the redheaded photographer.

He huddled in closer. 'Whatever kind of deal you've struck with Preston...'

'Deal I've struck with Preston?' she repeated, frowning. 'How could I strike a deal with Preston? Number one—I haven't got anything to deal with, and number two—I can't stand the guy.'

'Come on, Stacey. We didn't leave on good terms. Yet you "convinced" Preston to sell. For what? What was it you hoped to get out of it? All I'm saying is that I'll...'

He looked at her, watching as the confusion in her eyes gave way to understanding. And suddenly his heart pounded in his throat. *He got it.*

'Stacey, I assumed you'd pitched in with Preston. I thought maybe he'd—he'd given you an offer you couldn't refuse...'

She closed her eyes. She bowed her head.

'If I hadn't heard you say those words myself I don't think I'd have believed them.'

She lifted her chin. Shook her head.

'But you did. You said them.'

'Stacey, I'm sorry—I just couldn't see why you would still want to help out after what happened.'

'Wow... You think you know a guy and then...'

'Look, all I know is that one minute he was turning me on a spit and the next he was practically shoving the keys at me. And on his way to meet *you*. To take you to dinner to say thanks. What was I *supposed* to think?'

'I don't know, Marco, I really don't. Maybe that

old friends can do one another a good turn *without* there being a dirty motive?'

She stepped back from him, shaking her head as if she still couldn't really believe her ears.

'For your information, my motive was that even though it hadn't worked out between us we still had enough history for me to think that if all it took from me was a phone call, it was worth it to get you back something you wanted so badly.'

'Stacey. You've got to understand that—'

'I think we're through, Marco. I don't think I want to gather any more history with you. And just so we're clear—I've got a job here.'

She unbuttoned her jacket and he saw she was wearing the yellow gingham dress that was Betty's uniform.

'And I'll be living on-site while I lease out the house. My mother's moving to Canada. She's signed our house over to me and I've decided to stay. You might...' She nodded at the crowd, who were getting louder and more stupid with each passing second. 'You might want to find someplace else to hang out.'

She brushed past him and went up to the owner, who just happened to be his cousin. He watched as Mario embraced her warmly and then took her off down the hallway to his office.

'What the hell just happened there?'

Dante had appeared at his side. He put his hand on Marco's shoulder.

'I gotta hand it to you—you couldn't have played that worse if you'd tried. Shame,' he said as he slapped his back. 'I was betting on you two making it to the next round. But she won. Hands-down. And I wouldn't get up, if I were you. That was a knockout.'

CHAPTER FOURTEEN

STACEY CLOSED THE door on the last customers and locked it. She straightened the tablecloth on the console table in the vestibule and turned off the lamp. She walked back into the restaurant and began to stack chairs, making a mental note to order more upholstery fabric. Maybe even change the look. Nothing too different, but the place could do with a refresh.

In the kitchen she could hear voices and the muffled sounds of the kitchen porters putting away the dishes and clearing up before the whole thing started all over again tomorrow. Tomorrow was Sunday, still high season, and the place would be packed out from doors opening at ten until doors closing at midnight.

Betty's was an institution, for visitors and locals alike. Sometimes she even hung out there herself when she wasn't working. But it was to be her first full Sunday off since starting back here all those weeks ago, and she was going to make the most of it.

She was going to get up early, put on her old jeans

and get some more work done on the new place. She'd already done the kitchen and the bedroom, the hallway and porch. She'd weeded the driveway and repointed the stones that marked off the flowerbeds and then replanted them.

Who'd have believed that in the space of a month she'd own *two* properties in Montauk? When the craft shop couple had got in touch with her mother to ask if she wanted to buy she'd called Stacey right away. So technically it was a joint mortgage, but Toronto John was one of the good guys, and he had helped them get a low-rate deal.

He was one of the good guys, all right. He was the best. She'd never known her mom happier. He adored her—that was clear. But more than that he *respected* her.

She poured herself a decaf and sat down to count the money. It had been a busy day and it was the first time she'd stopped in hours. Her legs were sore and her back was sore. She kicked off her shoes and wiggled her toes, then put her feet down flat on the tiled floor.

It felt so good.

It wasn't just her work ethic—she'd always been a worker—it was the fact that she was now living in her own place and getting things done in her own time, on her own terms. She knew that the owner, Mario, prized her no-nonsense attitude and that he trusted her implicitly. She also knew that he was thinking of selling up.

When he'd told her, a little sliver of anxiety had crept over her. Just when things were going well… Whoever bought the place might turn it on its head. Turn her out on her ear. All she could hope was that it would be far enough in the future that she was really back on her feet and had maybe another couple of properties to her name. It was a godsend that the locals liked to sell to one another. Being friendly cost little, and had already reaped so much.

She stacked some bills and folded them over. The decaf coffee wasn't hitting the mark, but she wasn't much in the mood for anything else. It was only a short drive round the pond to her new place, and then a shower and bed were the only two things that held any appeal whatsoever.

Bed and lying awake staring at the freshly painted ceiling. Thinking about Marco Borsatto. Wondering where he was and what he was doing—and who he was doing it with. Wondering what would have happened had she rolled over that night and played along in his little game. If she'd held out for a nice new tennis bracelet instead of taking a potshot at him.

He'd wanted them to get it together—that was for sure. And every day since, in her low moments, she'd cursed herself for not going along with it. They'd had it good. He was the best.

But he didn't have her back. He didn't trust her and he certainly didn't respect her. And she couldn't spend time with anyone who thought so badly of her—even if she'd shared more with him than any other person on this earth. Even if their chemistry was cosmic. Even if she 'got' him the way she knew she did. She understood him wholeheartedly—completely. She understood the boy he'd been and the man he'd become. And why.

But true love was a two-way street. And *his* version headed to a dead end.

At least he'd taken her at her word and found someplace else to hang out. Since the day and the hour she'd started in Betty's he'd been a total stranger. Of course she'd heard about him—he was the local hero, and the fact that they'd had a quick affair was nothing special. He'd had quick affairs with a heap of women far more beautiful, talented and rich than she.

So the stories had kept coming. Dinner with the American Ambassador in Rome, a royal wedding in some tiny principality in Europe. A win at some polo match in Argentina. You name it, the people of Montauk had heard about it. Heard about it and pored over every detail, dissecting it and congratulating themselves on the time *they* had done this with Marco or that with Marco.

What a guy he was. Everyone's hero.

Except hers.

So she'd be single? She was fine with that. Having a career was her passion now. That and trying to make friends—which she had. Some of the girls who worked here were nice, and she was getting really tight with Coral, a fashion photographer. She hung around with the catwalk girls but she was human. For starters she ate actual food. And drank beer with real calories. Smiled with warmth instead of teeth.

Yeah, there were some pretty amazing people in this town. But a day on her own tomorrow was exactly what she needed.

She stacked up all the bills and tucked them into the money box, opened the safe and locked it all away. She was quite alone now. The kitchen staff had gone and the place was quiet and dark. She slid her feet back into her shoes, lifted her cup and padded back through to the restaurant, turning off the remaining lamps one by one before she lifted the keys.

Betty's was situated in an old house, set back from the road and secluded amongst high hedges that muffled the sounds of traffic and the rolling, crashing waves. At this time of night the staff left by the side door—solid and heavy and fitted with brass latches and handles. It had no window and weighed so much that even opening and closing it took huge effort.

Stacey slid back the bolts and pulled it open, feeling the heat of high summer warm on her face. She stepped onto the slab steps and stood, breathing in the damp salty air. The night was clear, but it was hard to see, and she fumbled then dropped her keys. She could make out the gleam of brass at her feet, but just as she reached out to lift them a bright beam of light flooded the scene.

She jumped up and turned round. Twin beams from a car's headlamps were trained right at her.

The engine wasn't on. No one got in or out. She held her hand up to shield her eyes and called out, but she couldn't even make out what type of car it was. Suddenly she felt panic surge into her mouth. Was this a robbery? Would she have to go in to get the money? Did they have a gun?

Praying that her little pumps wouldn't fall off, she bounded down the three steps and began to run.

'Stacey! It's all right—it's me—stop!'

She heard the words and knew the voice and her steps faltered. Her ankle twisted as she landed and she yelped in pain. Seconds later Marco was there—right beside her.

'Stacey—stop—are you okay?'

She grabbed her ankle and hopped. He reached for her but she batted out at him with her hand to get him to back off. And she cursed him. 'Dammit, Marco, you scared me half to death. What are you doing, sitting there like a stalker?'

'I'm waiting for you. I wanted to talk to you. Stop hitting at me, Stacey,' he said, grabbing her wrist and shaking his head.

Her eyes were now seeing past the glare of the headlamps and properly taking in the figure of Marco. Tall, strong and impossibly handsome.

She tugged her arm free, but when she tried to walk she lost her footing as her ankle twisted in pain.

'Here,' he said, his deep voice cutting through the night.

And before she could squeal he had scooped her

up into his arms and was holding her pressed against his chest.

'And don't bother struggling. Just accept my help without a fight, for once in your life.'

She drew her mouth into a grimace and breathed in deep, ready to give him a piece of her mind, but as she did so she smelled him. She smelled the unique-ness of him—his skin, his cologne, his maleness. Her hand slid out and laid itself flat against his chest, against the muscle, hot and hard. She looked up and saw his face, outlined in the yellowy beam of light. The lines of his jaw were firm and strong, and the angle of his cheekbones was moulded from the per-fect mask of some bygone Roman emperor.

The pity was he *acted* like an emperor too.

She felt her anger rise up. Who on earth did he think he was? She tried to wriggle out of his grip to stand on her own two feet, but he held her tighter and leaned over to open the door.

'Do as you are told, Stacey. Now—sit,' he said, placing her gently into the passenger seat. 'And don't move.'

He closed the door and came around, slid inside himself and started up the engine.

'Well, here we are again,' he said. 'Driving away from the scene of an accident.'

'Caused by *you*,' she said.

She stared straight ahead, not trusting herself to look. Not trusting herself not to get all wrapped up in him all over again.

'What do you want, Marco? I've had a hard shift and I just want to get back to my place.'

He answered that by putting his foot down. He knew the road better than anyone, and she had no fear, but still the surge of speed from his powerful car made her adrenaline pump all the harder around her body.

'This isn't the way,' she said as he took the cut-off and started to drive away from her neighbourhood. 'I've moved. I'm on the other side of town.'

'I know where you are. But we're not going there.'

'You're heading to the Meadows, aren't you?'

He nodded, then put his chin down.

'Look, can't this wait? I'm off tomorrow. I'm too tired for anything now.'

'No, it can't wait,' he said.

He speeded up again on the two-mile-long stretch of road that led only to the Meadows, and then slowed as they neared the gates. Huge and heavy, they swung open and he nosed the car inside. Low lamps studded along the edges of the driveway suddenly began to glow in sequence in a crescent before them.

Stacey sat up at the fairytale display. 'You brought me here to see your place at night? Okay. I get it. It's beautiful,' she said. 'But you overestimate my interest, Marco. We're nothing to do with one another any more. You should show it to someone who really cares. I'm only interested if you pay me, remember?'

'I wouldn't rule that out,' he said, keeping his eyes dead straight on the road.

Ahead the lamps became lit at the farthest corner of the drive, and there at the end stood the magnificence of Sant'Angelo's. All around it soft light sank from the eaves like sheer golden drapes to the ground, illuminating the stonework and the exquisite planters. High, wide windows—at least twenty on each side—pronounced the grandeur of the building. The entrance itself was wide, but welcoming, with a broad arch leading to a series of inner arches and finally to two heavy wooden doors.

'Wow,' said Stacey, despite herself. 'You really have pulled it off.'

'I'm happy you think so,' said Marco.

He slowed the car and crawled the last hundred yards to park at a broad sweep of steps.

'I knew it was beautiful but I don't remember it being like this. This is something else.'

'It was never like this before. I've had quite a lot done.'

They both stared up at it through the car's windscreen. The upper floor looked every bit as imposing as the ground.

'It's been all over Betty's about the work being done, but nobody seemed to know what, exactly.'

'That's a surprise. Must be the first time ever that word didn't get out in Montauk. Wait,' he said, opening his door and skirting the car to join her.

Stacey reached down to her ankle, absentmindedly rubbing her hand around it. It was swollen—there was no doubt. Unlikely she'd be climbing up any ladders with a paintbrush tomorrow.

Marco was at her side and the door was opened. He reached inside to scoop her up under her legs.

'Hey, Marco, this is stupid—' she began.

'Stacey once—just *once*—would you give it a rest?'

She was up and in his arms, smoothly and swiftly held against him.

She put her arms around his neck and scowled. 'It's late, it's dark, you scared the living daylights out of me and you expect me to be happy? After the last time we met?'

'Be happy for *me*, honey. Hmm...?'

Stacey looked up at him sharply. He never used terms of endearment or sweet little monikers—*ever*.

'Are you feeling all right?'

He shrugged her closer to his body, beamed a big smile down at her. 'Never better...never better.'

Something inside Stacey began to flutter to life. Some dark, gloomy corner of her heart suddenly brightened. She held on a little tighter.

As he walked them up the steps she noticed stone sconces, their quivering flames dancing in the light breeze. Night jasmine wafted from the planters, and the air was warm and thick with summer. As they neared the doors they opened automatically, allowing them a glimpse of what lay behind.

Marco stepped forward, and then paused on the threshold.

'I'll take it from here myself,' said Stacey.

The significance of being carried into a house by a man who wasn't her husband wasn't lost on her. She was done with any and all of those sorts of notions. She was on her own and she was better off that way.

He hesitated as she pushed back, and then relented and released her. She slid down his body, stifled a yelp when she put weight on her foot. But it wasn't broken, and she'd endured worse, so she hobbled forward and then straightened up and stepped through the doors.

Inside, the house was even more impressive. Although it was hundreds of years old he had installed clean, modern touches, with light flooding from cupolas on the ceiling and glass panels along one wall. The sweeping central staircase had been renovated, but its grandeur remained. Stacey's eyes scanned the vast hallway and the corridors leading off on either side. Polished floors, beautiful rugs and subtle lighting lent an atmosphere of modernity to its ancient dimensions.

'What do you think?'

Marco looked down at her and smiled. His eyes twinkled and his whole face glowed with pleasure. Her heart lit up with joy for him.

'Oh, Marco,' she said. 'I truly am happy for you. You got your house back and it was worth every second of your time and effort.'

She looked from one velvety brown eye to the other and almost burst with happiness. He was beaming with pride and she was beaming with pride *for* him.

'Come on—I'll show you round,' he said.

He took her hand and she walked as carefully as she could inside.

'When do you move in?' she asked. 'Or have you already? The gossips were quite sure you weren't going to live here—that it would be too full of memories.'

He laughed at that.

'At one point I might have agreed with them. Right up until last week, in fact.'

He paused at the doorway to a large sitting room, mostly open-plan. Although the night's darkness reflected the room back on itself, through sheets of glass she could see out across the lit terrace to a pool beyond.

'It struck me—even before I got the news that Preston had sold it to me—that I was trying to close a deal that deep down didn't really matter to me. It was all about the past—about getting back something I thought was important—instead of being about the future. At the end of the day we're all living on borrowed land. Before the Borsattos were the Dutch and the English. And the natives before them. And that doesn't even begin to take account of the wildlife.'

'I know. You were protecting your family name—we all got that,' she said simply. She'd learned to tune out of some of the conversations that had infested Betty's.

'What do you think? Do you remember these?'

Stacey drew her gaze back from the spectacular outdoors and followed his nod. There above a long sleek stainless steel stove, set into the wall, sat the three huge prints from his Atlantic City apartment.

She stepped forward. Smiled.

'Hey, yes! The lovely sky prints. Your saving grace in that antiseptic apartment.'

Then she looked around and smiled.

'You have some lovely things, Marco. Beautiful.' She moved around awkwardly on her foot, but it was fine, and she drew her fingers along a mauve velvet antique roll-top sofa, silk and satin cushions in the colours of saris from an Indian stall. The pale walls and light wood floors carried the little splashes of colour and old meeting new so well.

'Wow. It's beautiful. I *love* your colours. The whole vanilla look has—gone!'

She looked round to see how he would take that, but he was smiling.

'Yeah. That was the old Marco. You really like it?'

She nodded, looking round, taking in more details. 'I do—I really do. I'm impressed. Your designer has totally nailed it.'

'It was you who inspired it.'

Stacey let those words land just as lightly as it seemed they were said. She danced her eyes across all of the other things she could see. Little pieces of glass, a statue of a Hindu god, cashmere throws…

'You pointed out that the apartment wasn't a home—it didn't have any soul.'

'Well, I didn't mean to offend you. I was only trying to say that you seemed to be playing it safe.'

'I've been playing it safe for too long. In my personal life too.'

At that she paused. 'What are you saying, Marco?'

'I miss you, Stacey. You light me up. You bring colour into my world. It's so dull and lonely without you.'

Instantly she felt her eyes burn. The shock of hearing those words had torn open the old wound. The layers of time and grief, of work and struggle, all her attempts at self-love—lifted up like so much wet tissue. She was as sore underneath as she'd ever been. All those weeks and the scar could be lifted with four little words.

But they weren't the four little words she needed to hear. She wasn't going to let all that care and effort go to waste. He wasn't going to walk back into her life and say a bunch of stuff that meant nothing. She was *not* going to get carried away on another infatuation. Particularly one with Marco Borsatto.

She turned her head, pursed her lips, steeled herself.

'I didn't think I could, but I want to try to have a relationship with you,' he said.

She wished she had something to cauterise the

pain—something that would numb her against him for ever. An operation to seal over her bleeding heart. But all she had were words.

'And that's what you mean by "playing it safe" for too long? Having a relationship with me would be taking a walk on the wild side? Flying by the seat of your pants?'

He walked towards her. She could see him in the window.

'Can we have a conversation *without* an attack, Stacey? I want to explain how I feel.'

'Marco, it's three in the morning. You bring me here—and I still don't really know why after the last time we met—and you think we can have a conversation about how you *feel*? Have you thought for one minute how *I* feel? How I felt when you thought I was going to lose you your deal? When you thought I was holding out for more than a one-night stand? Or, worst of all, when you practically accused me of becoming the new Mrs Preston Chisholm? Did you stop for one single moment to see things from *my* point of view?'

'I know I messed up. I know I'm suspicious of people. But you can't blame me for that. The world I live in is stuffed full of piranhas trying to take a bite. I can't trust *anyone* any more.'

'But all of a sudden you feel you can trust *me*? You think I might not actually want to jump into bed with a man I clearly despise just to get you back for rejecting me?'

'I'm sorry—truly sorry. I was out of my mind with jealousy. I wanted you, but I didn't *want* to want you—do you understand? I find it hard to have faith in people. And you— You did it to me once before, Stacey. I know it shouldn't matter, and I tried not to let it get in the way, but it *hurt* me, dammit. It really hurt me.'

She stared at him now as she'd stared at him once before. That accusation, those stupid words that had caused them both so much pain, there before them. Ugly and sick. And completely devoid of truth.

'It didn't happen,' she said slowly, her voice a whisper. 'None of it happened.'

'What do you mean, Stacey?'

He eyed her warily. She almost despaired of going on with it. Who would believe that she would lie about such a thing and let that lie persist year after year? Who would believe that her explosive toxic anger could make her life spin off course? And his too, it now seemed.

She swallowed, started again.

'I never slept around back in high school. I never slept with anyone until I had a couple of boyfriends when I got to Atlantic City. And I never slept with anyone since then except you.'

He frowned. He shook his head. He paced and threw his hands up in the air.

'What are you trying to say? That you made it all up? What possible reason would you have for acting like that? That's insane. You messed up *my* life and *your* life because of that?'

'I didn't make it up—the town made it up. Those gossips made it up. Your so-called friends. And you chose to believe them over me.'

'I didn't believe them until you confirmed it. I didn't *want* to believe them! I wanted *you*! You and only you. And then you ran away and had the whole town out looking for you. Dammit, Stacey. I can't get my head around this. Why didn't you tell me sooner?'

She felt like an idiot now. It sounded so lame.

'I did try, Marco. Twice! But you didn't want to go over the past.'

He walked to the windows, stood staring out, battered his hand on the glass.

'But you could have *persuaded* me to listen! I still don't get it. Who *does* something like that?'

She watched him—his strong back and proud stance. His head was up and he was staring out across the land that he had travelled the globe and built up an empire for.

'I was sixteen. I wasn't thinking straight.' It was all she could say in defence.

'But you were old enough to know what you wanted. What you didn't want. So what was your motivation, Stacey? I understand theirs. They were jealous of us. Jealous of you.'

'No one was jealous of *me*, Marco—they *hated* me.'

He spun round, stood framed in the window against the glimmer of grey morning.

'If they hated you it was because you wouldn't let

them in. You gave out this air of being better than everybody else.'

'That's insane. I never thought I was better than anyone. All I wanted was to be like everyone else. I wanted to live in a nice house and have nice clothes and all those stupid things that seem important when you're young.'

'Stupid things like a father? I *know* you, Stacey. I know how that hurt you. I know you adored him and he left you. I know how you felt because I felt the same. Different circumstances, but the same thing.'

'It's not the same. My dad left because he was a loser and my mom couldn't take it any more. She stood up to him, but she let me go on thinking he was a good guy. She thought she was doing the right thing, but now all I feel is confusion. No one asked me how I felt. *Still* no one asks me how I feel. You've laid all this at my feet but I don't know what to do with it. I don't know who I am any more. Don't you *get* it?'

Across the room dawn was beginning to dust its light here and there. The early-rising birds were waking up. In another few hours the world would be fully roused and ready for the day ahead. All over this town and others people would be standing at the crossroads of their life, wondering which way to turn.

If she made the wrong decision now she might waste another ten years of her life—maybe more. Her mother had taken the wrong turning once and look what had happened.

'Yes, I get it,' he said. 'Come here,' he added, opening his arms and beckoning her towards him. 'Come here, sweetheart, and let's get past all the hurt. Come here and let me show you how much I love you.'

She stood in a column of disbelief, unmoving. He'd said the words her soft little heart had yearned to hear since the day she'd first laid eyes on him that summer she'd worked in Betty's. Since that day he'd left the crowd to walk her home while she slung insults at him and mocked his clothes and his hair and his money and everything she could because the likes of *her* didn't mix with the likes of *him*. And he'd put up with it and come back to walk her home the next day, and the next, until she'd finally believed that he wasn't teasing her. And then she'd told him of her dad and her mom and her fears and her hopes and dreams. And he'd told her of his.

When she didn't move he started to pace towards her.

'You're going to make me crawl for you, aren't you? I will, Stacey. I'll do it.'

He was smiling, but still she stood.

'Come on, honey. You can give in. You know we're dynamite together—all I want to do is prove it to you. You *know* me. Better than anyone ever knew me. Better than my mom or dad. Better even than I do myself. You know how I used to be. I can be that person again—with *you*. You bring out the real me.'

She was transfixed.

'Say it again,' she said.

He stopped. His eyes twinkled and his smile deepened.

'I love you, Stacey. I love you more than I ever thought possible.'

The splashes of dawn that dressed the room now merged into a vibrant morning. Outside the dewy grass began to hum under the warmth of a still sleepy sun.

What a day it was going to be.

Marco crossed the Indian rug, passed the low mosaic table with its curled legs, upon which flickered three fat candles, their pretty flames feebly battling the ever-decreasing night. His eyes locked onto hers. She felt his arms, his strength as he lifted her. She held onto his neck as he carried her. She sensed his heart pounding as hers was pounding too.

She knew she had finally come home.

* * * * *

If you enjoyed
THE ITALIAN'S VENGEFUL SEDUCTION,
why not explore the first part of Bella Frances's
CLAIMED BY A BILLIONAIRE duet?

THE ARGENTINIAN'S VIRGIN CONQUEST
Available now!

#3533 HER SINFUL SECRET
The Disgraced Copelands
by Jane Porter

Logan finds herself at Rowan Argyros's mercy when he discovers their secret daughter, but she cannot forget how he took her virginity and heartlessly rejected her. Rowan longs to claim her—but will her craving for his touch persuade her into marriage?

#3534 THE PRINCE'S NINE-MONTH SCANDAL
Scandalous Royal Brides
by Caitlin Crews

When personal assistant Natalie Monette discovers her secret identical twin, Princess Valentina, they decide to swap lives. Suddenly, her "fiancé" Crown Prince Rodolfo finds himself feeling a desire he cannot understand...until he discovers who's carrying the consequence of their passion!

#3535 THE DRAKON BABY BARGAIN
The Drakon Royals
by Tara Pammi

When Princess Eleni is offered a convenient marriage by Drakon's biggest investor, Gabriel Marquez, she strikes her own deal—she'll get a child of her own, he'll get a mother for his daughter. Except neither had predicted the fire that rages between them...

#3536 THE GREEK'S PLEASURABLE REVENGE
Secret Heirs of Billionaires
by Andie Brock

The last person Calista wants to see is Lukas Kalanos, who stole her innocence and left her with much more than a broken heart. On discovering her child is theirs, Lukas's pleasurable plans of revenge become a hunger to make her his!

YOU CAN FIND MORE INFORMATION ON UPCOMING HARLEQUIN® TITLES, FREE EXCERPTS AND MORE AT WWW.HARLEQUIN.COM.

HPCNM0517RB

HARLEQUIN

Presents®

Next month, look out for *The Prince's Nine-Month Scandal* by Caitlin Crews, the first part of her sinfully exciting new duet, Scandalous Royal Brides!

Natalie and Valentina cannot believe their eyes…they're the very image of one another, so similar they could be identical twins. They agree to swap identities for six weeks—but what will happen when the alpha heroes closest to them uncover the outrageous truth?

Natalie Monette's life is transformed by meeting Valentina—but Valentina is unhappily engaged to the supremely arrogant Crown Prince Rodolfo. Natalie's plan is to put arrogant Rodolfo in his place…until she's enticed by the heat between them!

Prince Rodolfo can't understand why, having *never* felt any desire for his betrothed, he now can't keep his hands off this captivating woman. But scandal abounds when he discovers who he's shared such passion with…and that she's carrying his heir!

Don't miss

The Prince's Nine-Month Scandal

Available June 2017

And discover Princess Valentina and Achilles Casilieris's story

The Billionaire's Secret Princess

Available July 2017

Stay Connected:

www.Harlequin.com

 /HarlequinBooks

 @HarlequinBooks

 /HarlequinBooks

HP06068

SPECIAL EXCERPT FROM

♦ HARLEQUIN
Presents.

*Ruthless Prince Adam Katsaros offers Belle a deal—
he'll release her father if she becomes his mistress!
Adam's gaze awakens a heated desire in Belle. Her
innocent beauty might redeem his royal reputation—but
can she tame the beast inside...?*

Read on for a sneak preview of
THE PRINCE'S CAPTIVE VIRGIN,
the first part of **Maisey Yates's**
ONCE UPON A SEDUCTION... *trilogy.*

"You really are kind of a beast," Belle said, standing up. Adam caught her wrist, stopped her from leaving.

"And what bothers you most about that? The fact that you would like to reform me, that you would like for your time here to mean something and you are beginning to see that it won't? Or is it the fact that you don't want to reform me at all, and that you rather like me this way? Or at least, your body likes me this way."

"Bodies make stupid decisions all the time. My father wanted my mother, and she was a terrible, unloving person who didn't even want her own daughter. So, forgive me if I find this argument rather uncompelling. It doesn't make you a good person, just because I enjoy kissing you. And it doesn't make this something worth exploring."

She broke free of him and began to walk away, striding down the hall, back toward her room. He pushed away from the table, letting his chair fall to the floor, not caring enough to right it as he followed after Belle.

He caught up to her, pivoting so that he was in front of her. She took a step backward, then to the side, butting up against the wall. Then he caged her between his arms, staring down at her. Her blue eyes were glittering, her breasts rising and falling rapidly with each breath.

"This is the only thing worth exploring. Not what could be, but what you have. The fire that burns between you and another person. For all you know, in the days since you've been here the entire world has fallen away. And if we were all that was left…would you not regret missing out on the chance to see how hot we could burn?"

She shook her head. "But the world hasn't fallen away," she said, her trembling lips pale now, a complete contrast to the rich color they had been only moments ago. "It's still there. And whatever happens in here will have consequences out there. I will help you, Adam, but I'm not going to give you my body. I'm not going to destroy that life that I have out there to play games with you in here. You're a stranger to me, and you're going to remain a stranger to me. I can pretend. I can give you whatever you need when it comes to making a statement for your country. But beyond that? I can't."

Then she turned and walked away, and this time, he let her go.